HOTHEADED ABOUT HOLLYWOOD

"I *had* noticed that you've been spending all your time with him," John said pointedly, pressing his lips into a tight line.

Lisa clenched her hands in annoyance. "Why shouldn't we? We're his technical advisers for the movie. Not to mention his friends," she said. She tried to keep her voice calm, but she could hear it quavering.

"His *best* friends, from what I can tell," John shot back.

"Skye has a lot of friends," Lisa said hotly. "He's a friendly person—which you would have noticed this afternoon if you hadn't been so bent on insulting him."

"That Hollywood pretty boy could use a couple of insults to take him down a peg or two!" John retorted.

THE SADDLE CLUB

by Bonnie Bryant

Saddle up and ride free with Stevie, Carole and Lisa. These three very different girls come together to share their special love of horses and to create The Saddle Club.

THE SADDLE CLUB

CUTTING HORSE

BONNIE BRYANT

BANTAM BOOKS
TORONTO • NEW YORK • LONDON • SYDNEY • AUCKLAND

THE SADDLE CLUB : CUTTING HORSE
A BANTAM BOOK : 0 553 50454 1

First published in USA by Bantam Skylark Books
First publication in Great Britain

PRINTING HISTORY
Bantam edition published 1997

"The Saddle Club" is a trademark of Bonnie Bryant Hiller.
The Saddle Club design/logo, which consists of riding crop
and a riding hat is a trademark of Bantam Books.

"USPC" and "Pony Club" are registered trademarks of The United States
Pony Clubs, Inc., at The Kentucky Horse Park, 4071 Iron Works Pike,
Lexington, KY 40511-8462, USA

Copyright © 1996 by Bonnie Bryant Hiller

With thanks to the management and staff at Snowball Farm
Equestrian Centre for their help in the preparation of the cover

Bantam Books are published by Transworld Publishers Ltd,
61–63 Uxbridge Road, Ealing, London W5 5SA,
in Australia by Transworld Publishers (Australia) Pty Ltd,
15–25 Helles Avenue, Moorebank, NSW 2170,
and in New Zealand by Transworld Publishers (NZ) Ltd,
3 William Pickering Drive, Albany, Auckland.

Printed and bound in Great Britain by
Cox & Wyman Ltd, Reading, Berkshire.

*I would like to express my special thanks
to Caitlin Macy for her help
in the writing of this book.*

"WATER, SPONGES, SADDLE soap, metal polish, oil, rags—I now pronounce us ready to clean tack," Carole Hanson said. Bridle in hand, she sat down on the floor of the tack room at Pine Hollow Stables.

One of her two best friends, Stevie Lake, sat down beside her. "You forgot the toothbrush and toothpaste," Stevie said.

"Toothbrush and toothpaste?" Carole asked.

Stevie nodded. "For the bits," she explained. "Believe me: Three out of four horses surveyed preferred the taste

1

of cool mint gel to the taste of metal polish. Starlight and Belle included."

Carole laughed. Starlight, a bay gelding, was her horse, and Belle, a half-Arabian, half-Saddlebred mare, was Stevie's. "I guess that's the least we can do for them, considering we won't see them for a week," Carole commented. It was summer vacation, and she, Stevie, and their other best friend, Lisa Atwood, were leaving the next morning for a week's trip out West.

"So I guess we should clean Lisa's tack, too, huh?" Stevie asked, the slightest note of reluctance creeping into her voice. Despite being horse-crazy like Carole and Lisa, Stevie wasn't known for her love of barn work like tack cleaning and stall mucking.

Carole looked sternly at her. "Now, Stevie—" she began.

"I know, I know: Saddle Club rule number two, right?" Stevie guessed.

"Right," Carole confirmed. She didn't have to say more. The three girls had started The Saddle Club, so they knew its rules cold. Besides, there were only two: Members of the club had to be (1) horse-crazy and (2) willing to help one another out in any kind of situation. Rule number two was the reason Carole and Stevie were going to have to clean Lisa's tack.

2

"I still don't understand why Lisa didn't show up for the good-bye ride," said Stevie, soaping the reins of her bridle.

"It is weird," Carole agreed. "It's not like Lisa to miss an appointment—even an appointment with us."

Whenever the girls went on a trip, they knew that no matter how much fun they had, they would miss their horses. So they always liked to take a long last trail ride before they left. Carole would ride Starlight, Stevie would ride Belle, and Lisa would ride Prancer, an ex-racehorse. Unlike Carole and Stevie, Lisa didn't have her own horse, but she had trained Prancer for so long that it almost seemed like the same thing.

"Maybe Lisa's mother dragged her to the mall for some new Western riding outfits," Stevie suggested.

"It wouldn't be the first time," Carole said, shaking her head. Mrs. Atwood liked Lisa to look nice all the time, in perfectly matched outfits, so she was constantly taking her shopping for new clothes.

"At least we'll all be together tomorrow morning for the flight out," Carole continued. "And I can hardly wait to see Kate and the ranch and everyone. Aren't you excited?"

To Carole's surprise, Stevie didn't answer right away. She wrung her sponge out thoughtfully and waited for a

3

minute or two before replying. "I guess so," she said finally.

"You *guess* so?" Carole repeated, incredulous. "Wait a minute. Is this Stevie Lake I'm talking to? School's out, you're about to spend a week on your favorite dude ranch with your two best friends, riding and hanging out to your heart's content, and you *guess* you're excited?" Carole could hardly believe her ears. The girls had taken a number of trips out West to visit an old friend—and an out-of-town Saddle Club member, Kate Devine. Kate's parents owned and operated a dude ranch called the Bar None. The Saddle Club always had a wonderful time there.

Stevie smiled at Carole. "You're right. I know it's going to be great. But sometimes I worry that if we *plan* to have fun, we won't. You know?"

"Yes," Carole replied. "I know what you mean. Every time we've gone out West, something incredibly exciting has happened, and it's always been something we didn't plan."

"Exactly," said Stevie. "Like the time the Devines needed us to help them save the ranch."

"And the trip when we helped catch the cattle rustlers," Carole chimed in. "Yup. We've had our share of adventures out there. But I think this trip will be great, too."

4

"Okay. I just don't want to curse things by *planning* all the fun we're going to have," Stevie insisted.

"Well, then we'll just have to sit here and clean tack in silence because that's all I can think about!" Carole said.

Just then the tack room door swung open and Lisa burst into the room. She stood there, red-faced and panting, for several minutes. Carole and Stevie stared at her. Finally she caught her breath enough to speak. "I just got off the phone," she managed to blurt out. "And you'll never, ever guess who just called me!"

"Skye Ransom," Stevie said, trying to think of the most unlikely person for Lisa to get a call from. Skye Ransom was a teenage movie star whom the girls had met on a trip to New York.

Lisa's jaw dropped. "You guessed!" she cried indignantly. "And here I was planning to keep you wondering for hours."

"*Skye Ransom?*" Stevie and Carole repeated incredulously. Stevie had been joking—she hadn't believed for one second that Skye was the person who had called.

Even though the girls kept in touch with Skye, he didn't usually call out of the blue to chat. He was a very busy professional. He flew all over to make movies, and the rest of the time he was occupied with leading the glamorous life of a young star in Hollywood.

5

"He wanted to say hi?" Carole asked doubtfully.

Lisa grinned. "I guess you could say that. He did tell me to say hi to you guys," she said. "Of course, I told him that he could wait"—Lisa paused dramatically—"and do that in person!"

"In person?" Stevie and Carole cried. Now they were utterly confused. Unless Skye planned to show up in Willow Creek, Virginia, that night, they would miss him. They were due to fly out early the next morning with Kate's father. Frank Devine was a retired Marine Corps pilot who flew a private plane part-time. The girls tried to time their visits so that they could hitch free rides with him.

"Lisa," Carole asked gently, "have you, um, by any chance, forgotten that our trip starts tomorrow?"

"Yes," Stevie said, chuckling, "unless Skye's planning on checking into the Bar None, I don't see how we're going to meet up with him."

"Oh, he's not planning on checking into the Bar None," Lisa said.

"Well then?" said Stevie.

"He's already there!"

Stevie and Carole looked at one another wildly. "You mean Skye Ransom just happens to be taking a vacation

6

at the Bar None the same week we are?" Carole demanded.

Lisa started to giggle. "Not exactly."

Stevie stood up and put her hands on her hips. Obviously, Lisa had news—good news—but she was making them extract it from her piece by piece. "All right, Atwood, out with it! What's the story?"

"Okay, okay. It's too good to keep secret. Skye Ransom is filming a movie at the Bar None!" Lisa cried.

It took a minute for her words to sink in. Then Stevie and Carole let out a huge whoop. Before they could barrage her with questions, Lisa sat down with them on the floor and told the whole incredible story. "It all started a few months ago, but I didn't want to tell you in case it didn't work out. Skye called me and asked if I could recommend a ranch where they could film a Western he's going to be in. Naturally, I said the Bar None. But I never heard anything more about it. I thought maybe the movie got canceled."

Stevie and Carole nodded. So far, everything made sense. Skye had called Lisa because he knew her a bit better than he knew them. Lisa had hung out with him on a trip she'd taken to Los Angeles with her mother. The fact that Skye hadn't called her back was normal, too. As he had told them, Hollywood was a crazy place. Movie projects got abandoned all the time, sometimes even when they were far along. So it was no wonder that Lisa hadn't given the conversation a second thought.

"Anyway," Lisa continued, "this morning I was dressed to come riding when the phone rang. I picked up, and a voice said, 'Last night I watched the sun set over the Rockies.' It was Skye! It turns out that the producers flew out to see the ranch, and they loved it. I guess the Devines were thrilled, too. They're getting a lot of money, and it will be great publicity for the Bar None. The filming started yesterday!"

"You mean Kate's known about this for weeks and she hasn't said a thing?" Stevie asked. She was amazed that anybody could keep such a fantastic secret.

"She wanted it to be a surprise. But the minute I got off the phone with Skye, I called the Devines. Kate was really mad that Skye had broken the news, because she wanted it to be a big surprise when we got there. But she can't wait for us to come," Lisa finished.

"Well, I guess the no-fun curse is off!" Carole said. At Lisa's puzzled expression, she explained Stevie's fear that any plan to have fun would backfire.

Lisa laughed. In a mock-serious tone, she said, "Don't get any ideas that this trip is going to be all fun and games. I did tell you we're going to be working very hard, didn't I?" When Carole and Stevie shook their heads, Lisa explained. "The three of us have very important jobs. Skye's made us his official technical advisers on equine matters."

"Huh?" Stevie said.

"We make sure he can ride," Lisa translated.

"Considering how we met him, I think that's appropriate," Carole said, laughing. The girls had met Skye in New York City's Central Park because he'd fallen off his horse trying to pretend he knew how to ride during a shoot. They'd rescued him and the horse and coached him so that he could ride well enough to get by in the movie.

Stevie liked the idea of being a technical adviser so much that she let out another whoop. "Yippee-hi-yi-yay!" she yelled, getting into the Western spirit. "The Saddle Club goes to the Bar None and the Bar None goes Hollywood! We're going to have the best—" In the middle of her sentence, Stevie stopped. Out of the corner of her eye she saw the knob of the tack room door turning. She didn't have to guess who it was.

Sure enough, Max Regnery III poked his head in. Max was the owner of Pine Hollow Stables and the girls' riding instructor. "May I remind you three that you're not 'home

9

on the range' yet, but in an enclosed stable in Willow Creek, Virginia, where loud noises carry!" he barked.

The minute he was gone, Stevie started to whistle under her breath, a defiant look in her eye.

"What tune is that?" Lisa asked.

Stevie leaned forward and said, in a stage whisper, " 'Don't Fence Me In'!"

THE SMALL PLANE touched down in a perfect landing. As they shuttled along the runway, Stevie, Lisa, and Carole burst into spontaneous applause. They had started their trip at the crack of dawn and slept most of the way to Denver, but now that they were on the ground, they were buzzing with excitement.

"You girls can fly with me anytime," said Frank Devine, emerging from the cockpit a few minutes later.

"Does that mean we're welcome at the ole Bar None anytime, too?" Stevie asked.

"Absolutely. Although I have to warn you: The Bar

None might not look quite so 'ole' anymore. In fact, you might not recognize the place. It's been completely Hollywood-ized. Some days I forget I'm at a real ranch, it looks so much like a ranch *set*."

The girls laughed. With its neat buildings and acres of prairie, and with the Rockies rising in the distance, the Bar None did look like the kind of ranch a movie producer would dream up. That was why it was called the Bar None—Kate's parents had thought it was the prettiest ranch they had ever seen, bar none.

"Of course, around about feeding time, the horses remind me that they're real enough," Kate's father continued. "And we do try to feed the humans at regular hours, too," he added, with a sidelong glance at Stevie. Stevie's unquenchable appetite was well known to the Devines.

"Phew!" Stevie exclaimed. "I thought maybe I was going to have to make do with fake movie food or something."

"Nope. If we skimped on meals at the Bar None, my ranch hands would all go on strike, no doubt about it."

The girls gathered up their bags and followed Frank down the steps of the plane, through the airport, and out to the passenger pickup area, where someone from the ranch was going to meet them. As usual, Lisa had twice as much luggage as Carole and Stevie.

"I'll stow it in the bunkhouse the minute we get there," Lisa promised in response to their groans about the weight. No matter how hard she tried, Lisa never succeeded in keeping her mother away from her suitcases before a big trip. When Mrs. Atwood had heard that Skye Ransom was going to be at the ranch, she'd gone crazier than usual, adding dresses, skirts, and blouses to Lisa's overstuffed bags. She loved the fact that her daughter knew a real movie star, and she was always encouraging Lisa to look her best.

"You might not want to stow all of it," Stevie said teasingly. "You never know when you'll need to spruce up for a certain someone. Speaking of ranch hands . . ."

"Yes?" Lisa said innocently. She knew exactly what Stevie meant, but she also knew that Stevie was not about to let on, in front of Kate's father, that Lisa liked one of his ranch hands. Dark-haired and tall, John Brightstar was an American Indian and the son of the Devines' head wrangler, Walter Brightstar. John was about a year older than the girls. He worked on the ranch after school and in the summer. Lisa and he were friends, but they were a little more than friends, too. Lisa was looking forward to spending time with him on this trip.

Fortunately, Frank Devine was paying attention to the approaching cars and didn't seem to notice the pause in their conversation. "Here we go—here's the van now," he said.

The Saddle Club looked to see where he was pointing. "That's them?" Lisa asked. Instead of the usual dilapidated ranch truck or weathered station wagon, a deluxe dark green minivan pulled up to the curb.

Frank nodded proudly. "We bought it a month ago, after we signed the contracts with Hollywood. Officially, it's our 'airport pickup' van."

The minute the van had stopped, the passenger-side window was lowered, and Kate stuck her head out. "Pretty spiffy, huh?" she cried. She pointed at the neat white lettering on the side of the van, which read THE BAR NONE, followed by the ranch logo: $\overline{\text{o}}$

"Spiffy enough for Skye Ransom!" Carole replied.

"Are you sure it's not too posh for The Saddle Club?" Stevie joked.

"Absolutely not," Kate said, getting out of the van. "Don't forget: I'm a member, too."

"How could we forget?" Stevie demanded as she, Lisa, and Carole hugged their friend.

When Lisa disentangled herself from the hugging, she checked to see who else had come to the airport. Walter and John Brightstar had gotten out of the van and were leaning against it, talking with Frank. Delighted that John

14

had come to greet her instead of waiting at the ranch, Lisa went forward to give him a big hug. But at the last minute she stopped and shyly said, "Hi." There was something about John's manner that had made her change her mind about the hug.

"Hi, Lisa," John said in a subdued tone.

"How have you been? It's great to see you," Lisa said in a rush.

"I've been . . . okay, I guess," John said.

Lisa was surprised by his response. She had assumed that everybody on the ranch would be infected with the Hollywood bug the way The Saddle Club was. But John certainly didn't look thrilled—or sound it, either.

"All right. Troops in. Let's get on home to the ranch," Frank said, sounding like his old military self.

Lisa piled into the van with everyone else. She was sorry not to talk to John more, but it would be better to catch up with him later. If he was upset about something, he wouldn't want to talk about it in front of everyone.

"So what do you think of Skye?" Stevie asked Kate as soon as they were on the way.

"He's great!" Kate exclaimed. "He's such a nice guy, and he's so friendly and down-to-earth for a movie star. The day he arrived, he came right over to our house,

15

knocked on the door, and introduced himself to the whole family."

"That's just like Skye," Carole said. "You almost forget he's famous."

"Even Dad would agree with that," Kate said.

Frank looked back from the front seat. "I certainly would. That boy has impressed all of us."

"Has he met the horses yet?" Carole inquired.

Kate nodded. "Oh, yes. This morning he came over and borrowed Spot to practice on." With a giggle, Kate added, "I must say he looked pretty darn good on a horse, even though he's not an expert rider."

"Those blue eyes, those curly blond locks . . . ," Stevie murmured melodramatically.

"Okay, okay. We know what he looks like!" Carole protested.

"Look, I'm just glad to hear that everyone at the Bar None has joined the Skye Ransom Fan Club," Stevie said. "Because we've been members since the day we met him."

"You're lucky that you've gotten to know him so well," Kate said.

"Oh, we don't know him *that* well," Stevie said, her hazel eyes twinkling mischievously. "The only one of us who's really spent any quality time with Skye is Lisa."

"Quality time? Really?" Kate asked, eyebrows raised.

"Tell her, Lisa," Stevie prompted.

"It wasn't that big of a deal," Lisa muttered.

"Not that big of a deal? You were out in Los Angeles for a whole week with Skye, getting taken out every night as his date—"

"I wasn't *with* Skye," Lisa broke in. "I was with my mother."

"Yeah, but—" Stevie stopped abruptly as Carole elbowed her.

"We *all* like Skye, and that's the important thing," Carole said firmly. Silently she wished that Stevie would stop talking about Lisa's trip to California. Carole had noticed that during the conversation about Skye, Lisa had been silent. Obviously Lisa didn't want them to talk in front of John about how much she liked Skye. She was sensitive enough to realize that John might mind. Stevie hadn't picked up on that. And now she had made matters worse by bringing up Lisa's California trip. The purpose of the trip had been for Lisa to visit her aunt, who was sick. It was only by chance that she'd been able to see Skye, too. But John didn't know that—and, judging by her awkward expression, Lisa knew that he didn't know.

The rest of the ride home was quieter. Lisa and John stared out their windows. Carole changed the subject to horses, and she and Kate exchanged notes on Starlight and Kate's horse Moonglow. It was a relief when they finally arrived at the ranch.

Walter dropped the girls off in front of the bunkhouse where they always stayed. Before she got out, Lisa told John that she hoped they'd have time to talk later.

"I do, too," John said, "but I'm really busy. I—I'll have to see."

Lisa watched the van drive off. So far her reunion with John wasn't going the way she had expected. And she had no idea why.

FRANK DEVINE WAS RIGHT: The girls hardly recognized the place. The Bar None had been transformed into a Hollywood studio. Behind the bunkhouse and stables was a long row of trailers, and behind them, a smaller row of portable toilets. All over the ranch, roped-off sections divided the property. Huge sets of lights on wheels flanked different sections. And everywhere, there were people—people riding vehicles like golf carts from place to place, people dashing around with camera equipment, people laying out food on picnic tables, people talking on cellular phones, people running, people yelling, people arguing.

Stevie, Carole, and Lisa set their luggage down and just stared for several minutes.

18

"It's kind of a three-ring circus, isn't it?" said Kate.

"More like ten-ring!" Carole responded. "How are the horses holding up?"

The girls smiled. It was just like Carole to ask about the horses. She was always more concerned with their welfare than anyone else's.

"Why don't we go see for ourselves?" Kate suggested. "In fact, let's sneak out on a trail ride before somebody puts us to work!"

The girls didn't have to be asked twice. Within minutes they had dumped their bags in the bunkhouse, changed into jeans and boots, and headed out to the stable.

Lisa, Carole, and Stevie each had a favorite horse at the Bar None. Lisa's was a pretty bay mare called Chocolate. Carole rode Berry, a strawberry roan. Stevie rode Stewball.

Stewball was a very unusual horse. First there was his color. He was a skewbald, meaning he was white with irregular patches of a brownish chestnut color. But more than his color, it was his personality that made him unique. He was the stubbornest horse the girls had ever encountered. Anything he did, he did his way, from picking up a trot to rounding up cattle. Stevie had learned very quickly that it was hopeless for her to tell Stewball how to do something: He would just ignore her. And he

19

was such a great cutting horse and all-around Western mount that there was no reason to even *try* to tell him what to do. Chances were, he would be right and the rider would be wrong.

As the girls groomed the horses and tacked up, Lisa brought up John's sober mood. "I wish I knew what was irking him—if something was. Maybe I'm just being hypersensitive."

"It's all my fault," Stevie said. "I didn't even realize the conversation about Skye would upset John until everyone got so quiet."

"Don't worry about it," Lisa said. "That obviously didn't help things, but John was in a bad mood before that. He doesn't seem to be himself."

"That's not hard to believe," Kate said. "I can sympathize. Ever since Dad signed the deal with the studio, we've all been working twice as hard as we usually do. The people from Hollywood don't know anything about horses or ranch life. We practically have to hold their hands. And they keep getting in the way, and that makes it more difficult to get all the rest of our work done. John's probably so tired he can't see straight. We all are. Once we get a breather, John will snap back to normal."

20

"I guess you're right," Lisa said. "I just hope he snaps back in the next week."

Soon the horses were tacked up and ready to go. When the girls had first visited the ranch, it had been a challenge for them to get used to Western tack and the different riding style. But now they were confident in the horned saddles, and they really enjoyed the change from English riding.

One by one they led the horses from the barn into the beautiful, sunny day. Stevie inhaled loudly. "Even the air here is different," she said.

"Yeah," Kate said with a grin, "I hear it's better for barbecuing."

"Don't tempt me like that!" Stevie wailed. "I'd give my right arm for an old-fashioned Western barbecue!"

"Well, you just might be able to keep the arm and still have a barbecue," Kate said. "Dad's planning to have a huge cookout for the staff one night this week to boost morale."

"So I guess that means Stevie can have her barbecue and eat it too?" Lisa said.

Astride Berry, Carole spoke up. "Would you guys mind getting on your horses one of these days? Berry and I are raring to go."

As if in agreement, Berry raised her head and neighed loudly. Close by, another horse answered. The girls turned and saw Kate's old Appaloosa, Spot. Spot's rider raised his hand and waved. It was Skye! "Got room on your ride for a real dude?" he called.

3

"Wow, AM I GLAD to see you guys," Skye said. "I don't think I've spoken with anyone other than the director, the people in makeup, and the camera crew for forty-eight hours."

"So they're keeping you pretty busy, huh?" Stevie said. Everyone knew that when Skye was shooting a movie, fifteen- and twenty-hour days were not uncommon.

"I'll say! But I managed to get a couple of hours off this afternoon to practice on Spot here, so I figured I'd sneak over to the stables in case you all had arrived," Skye replied.

"You mean you actually guessed that you'd find The Saddle Club with the horses?" Kate asked.

"I did have a hunch," Skye said, flashing one of the grins that had made him a coast-to-coast heartthrob.

"It must be ESP," Lisa said.

The girls couldn't wait to hear what was new with Skye. But first they had to escape the distracting hubbub. They trotted to the trailhead and then slowed to a walk so that they could all hear one another.

"First of all, tell us about the movie," Lisa urged. "As your official technical advisers, we should know the plot and all the details."

Skye agreed happily. "Well, I guess you know by now that it's a Western. The name of it is *Cowboy Come Home*. It's a romance, too—about a young cowboy who rides a championship cutting horse. He falls in love with a city girl. I, um, play the cowboy."

"Sounds like a great part," Lisa responded. It was typical of Skye to downplay his success—like putting in an *um* before saying that he had the lead role.

"Yeah, I was really psyched when Frank found the part for me," Skye agreed. Frank Nelson was Skye's manager. He handled every part of Skye's career, from contracts to salary negotiations to publicity.

"Ever since *City Cowboy*," Skye continued, "I've been

24

trying to find another riding movie, but they don't come along too often. I loved watching Westerns as a kid, so that makes this part even better."

"I love Westerns, too," said Stevie. "Nothing beats a good John Wayne double feature."

"You're right about that. I've been rewatching some of my old favorites to get in the right frame of mind for *Cowboy Come Home*, and man, is he a master," Skye said reverently.

"So it sounds like everything is going well for you, Skye," Carole said. "That's great." She steadied Berry so that she could listen to Skye's response.

"Not so fast," Skye replied. "I'm actually having my share of problems."

"Even with the role of your dreams?" Stevie asked.

"That's just it," said Skye. "It *should* be the role of my dreams—especially in this setting. I love the idea of playing a real Western cowboy. Unfortunately, it's the cowboy stuff that's tripping me up."

"What do you mean? Your riding has improved so much," Carole said. She meant it, too. From the out-of-control beginner The Saddle Club had met, Skye had turned into a competent intermediate-level rider. He sat comfortably in the saddle, controlling Spot easily with his legs, seat, and hands.

25

"Thanks. I've worked on it out in L. A., and I feel more confident now," said Skye. "But the thing is, in the movie I'm supposed to be an amazing rider—a champion. There are only a few scenes where I actually have to show my skills, but so far I haven't been able to pull them off. There are a couple of herding and cutting scenes that aren't working at all. I can't keep control of the herd of cattle and my horse at the same time."

The Saddle Club knew that cutting cattle was a specialized skill. The horse and rider had to isolate a cow in a very short time. Then they had to keep the cow from rejoining the herd. Successful cutting was an elegant exercise. In rodeo competitions, it was considered one of the most intellectual tests because the horse and the rider had to anticipate the cow's moves.

"Could they use a stuntman?" Kate asked tentatively.

"They could," Skye answered. "Actually, that's just what the director wants to do. He keeps threatening me and saying he's going to call in a double, and I keep pleading with him not to. I just can't resign myself to the idea of having someone else do my riding scenes. It would be one thing if I had to leap from a burning building, but I *know* how to ride. I don't want my fans to find out that Skye Ransom was too pathetic to do his own scenes on horseback." Skye hesitated before he went on, more quietly, "The truth is, my last movie was a flop. I can't afford to have another. And doing my own riding might make the difference between a hit and a box-office failure."

"So the director just thinks you're not good enough yet?" Carole asked. She didn't want Skye to start worrying about his career. First they had to find out whether they could help him.

"Yes, but only because I told him. Boy, was that ever stupid," Skye said disgustedly. "That guy doesn't know the first thing about horses. In fact, he's half the problem. He keeps asking me to do all these things that are impossible—like making my horse stand absolutely still for five minutes so that they can get a good shot of a sunset."

"If he can't tell the difference, why don't you tell him you *are* ready?" Stevie asked. She was never above a few white lies to get something she was after.

Skye let out a troubled sigh. "I can't do that, either. The only thing more embarrassing to me than my fans' finding out that I didn't do my own riding would be for me to ride and look stupid. Some people won't know, but the ones who do will think, 'What a joke! That guy couldn't pass for a cowboy in a million years.' "

"Right. Like those perfume commercials where you see models galloping along a beach. They're always wearing the silliest dresses and practically falling off," Carole com-

27

mented. "I mean—not that you're practically falling off—"

Skye put up a hand to stop Carole from explaining. "That's exactly what I mean. This director wanted me to get my horse to rear up and paw the air every time I mounted."

"Just like the Lone Ranger and Silver," Stevie said, giggling.

"Tell me about it! And the only reason I wanted to do this movie was to get a chance to play a real cowboy. I never even thought about having a stuntman. . . ." Skye's voice drifted off unhappily.

"Don't worry, Skye. That's why we're here—to help you," Lisa said.

"Right. And I'm sure we'll be able to get your riding into shape for the movie in a week," Carole predicted.

"That's just it, though. We don't *have* a week. We're already behind schedule. The director wants to do the cutting scene on Wednesday in order to have time to do the other long shots before we fly back to L. A. on Saturday. That means I only have about three days to prepare," Skye explained.

"One week, three days—no matter what, we're going to get you ready," Carole promised. "Just as fast as we can. We'll start this afternoon, the minute you're free." She

28

didn't believe Skye's problems were as bad as he was making them sound. The movie that had flopped was probably unnerving him, that was all. It was like falling off at a horse show: Until a rider had proved herself again, at another show, she was haunted by the memory.

"Okay, Carole," Skye said, but he didn't sound convinced.

Lisa didn't like the worried edge to his voice. The Saddle Club could at least try to cheer him up temporarily. "What do you say we have a nice canter up this hill before we turn around and go back?" she suggested.

"I don't know about a canter," Skye said, his smile slowly returning, "but I'd love a nice lope!"

Lisa laughed. She had forgotten for a minute that in Western riding the gaits were called walk, jog, and lope instead of walk, trot, and canter. Happy that Skye had been the one to correct her, she nudged Chocolate into the faster pace.

The horses covered ground quickly, and soon they were at the top of the gently rising hill. Even from the slight elevation, the Western scenery was breathtaking. The prairie rolled on for miles, fading into the desert greens and browns—with the Rockies beyond. After silently taking in the beauty of the landscape, the five riders reluctantly turned around and headed back.

At the Bar None, the girls volunteered to untack Spot and put him away so that Skye wouldn't be late for the filming.

"Thanks a bunch, you guys," Skye said, dismounting neatly. "The last thing I need is for the director to think I'm slacking off." He handed his reins to Carole and turned to go, but Stevie's voice stopped him.

"Hey, wait!" she called. "You never told us how the movie ends!"

Skye winced. "I was afraid you'd ask me that. Okay: The cowboy gives up riding the range for the girl he loves."

All four girls groaned in unison. "Oh, no—really, Skye?" Carole asked.

Skye nodded. "I'm afraid so."

"But that's terrible!" Stevie protested.

"I know, I know—but hey, that's Hollywood!" Skye said.

AFTER PUTTING THE horses away and fixing themselves a late-afternoon snack in Kate's kitchen, the girls decided to walk over and check out the filming. Kate led them to a large roped-off area near one of the outer corrals. It was very crowded close to the set. Dozens of people were milling around. Kate threaded through the rows of onlookers until she reached the barrier rope.

"I don't know where the break in this rope is, but I see some chairs that look like they were set up for viewing," Kate said, pointing.

"Let's just duck under the rope, then," Stevie suggested, slipping underneath it as she spoke. Kate and Carole followed. Lisa was about to join them when a harsh voice coming over a bullhorn commanded, "Stop right where you are!"

Lisa had barely straightened up before a uniformed security guard was breathing down her neck. "What do you girls think you're doing?" he demanded. "This is a private filming session. Can't you read?" He pointed to the NO TRESPASSING signs hung at intervals all along the rope.

Shocked, Lisa looked to Kate for help.

Her blue eyes flashing, Kate drew herself up to her full height. "I am Kate Devine," she said.

"Kate who?" the guard asked.

"Kate Devine. The daughter of Frank and Phyllis Devine. We *own* the ranch."

The guard eyed her suspiciously. "All right," he said. "I guess you can watch. But I don't know about your friends."

"These aren't simply my friends," Kate informed him icily. "These are three personal friends of Skye Ransom, not to mention his technical advisers for the movie."

By now the guard looked a little nervous. "Really?"

"Really," Kate said flatly.

"Well, how come you weren't here an hour ago?" the guard asked.

"Because we were looking after Mr. Ransom's practice mount, of course," Stevie said in the coldest tone she could muster.

The guard shook his head. "All right, I give up. Go ahead in."

On their way to the seating area, Lisa, Stevie, and Carole laughed the incident off. But Kate was still upset.

"We did look like we were sneaking in," Stevie pointed out. "In fact, this may be the most wrong I've ever looked when I was right."

"I guess so," Kate said, "but I'm sick of being ordered around on my own property."

The seating area was a platform raised on scaffolding at one side of the set. A number of older people were watching. The girls climbed the steps and found a group of empty folding chairs near the back. As soon as they were seated, someone yelled, "Quiet on the set!" and then,

"Roll film!" The Saddle Club leaned forward in their seats to watch the action begin.

Off in the distance a horse and rider appeared and began to guide a small herd of cattle toward a corral. A dog skirted the herd, barking, helping the rider bring them forward. In a couple of minutes the girls could see Skye clearly.

Again Carole noticed how confident Skye looked. "He's ten times better than the last time we saw him," she whispered. "He won't need a double!"

Just then, as the herd neared the corral, one of the cows tried to dart away. Skye turned his horse to stop the cow. But instead of obeying, the horse balked and started to back up. "Cut!" a voice screamed.

A short, red-faced man charged onto the set. He ran up to Skye's horse and waved his fists in the air. "What do you think you're doing? You're supposed to stay to the right so we get the mountain backdrop in. If you cut left, all we see behind you are a couple of ugly buildings."

"But the cow ran left, so I had to follow her," Skye explained.

"Cow! Who cares about the cow? *You're* the star of this movie, Skye, not the cow! And the horse—try to make him prick up his ears! We want him to look like he enjoys this. Okay? Got it?"

Skye looked down at the director, visibly trying to control his reaction. "Yes, I've got it," he muttered.

Back on the viewing stand, the girls were indignant. It was clear from the exchange that the director knew nothing about any animals—and horses in particular.

"What was Skye supposed to do? Let the cow run away?" Carole asked, her dark eyes flashing angrily. Nothing annoyed her more than people who thought horses could be ridden like bicycles.

"I'm telling you, this is typical of their attitude," Kate said.

"You must be really tired of them," Lisa said sympathetically. "It's no wonder John's fed up too."

"Hey, speaking of John . . . ," Kate said, and pointed. Lisa turned and looked down. John was leaning against the platform scaffolding, watching the commotion between takes with a skeptical look.

Lisa stood up and called to him. She waited until he found her face in the crowd and then yelled, "Come up and watch with us!"

John motioned that he would. As he began to pick his way through the throng of assistants, grips, and camerapeople, the director's high, nasal voice pierced the air again. "Somebody better get me my coffee within ten seconds or heads are going to roll!"

34

Lisa saw a harried young woman thrust a paper cup into John's hand. "Take it to him! Quick!" she cried. John looked surprised, but he shrugged, walked forward, and handed it to the director.

"It's about time!" the little man screamed. "You think I have all day to wait for my coffee? Next time you get it to me fast, got it?"

John opened his mouth to protest, but before he could say anything, someone else screamed, "Clear the set! Everybody off the set! Quiet!" John looked shocked, then utterly disgusted. Instead of coming up and joining the girls, he ducked under the rope and disappeared into the crowd. Watching him stalk off, Lisa didn't know who annoyed her most—the woman with the coffee, the director, or John. With a frustrated sigh, she sat down to watch the retake.

The second take—and the third—didn't go any better than the first. The cattle were getting sick of being herded back and forth. Skye and the sheepdog had to work twice as hard to keep them moving in the right direction. The director's demands were only making things more difficult. But on the third take, Carole noticed something. It wasn't just the director who was giving Skye a hard time—his horse was, too. The horse didn't seem to know anything about cattle. He looked nervous and unsettled

35

and didn't show any of the signs of a good cutting horse. When Skye urged him closer, he shied and backed away.

"Who is Skye riding?" Carole whispered to Kate. She couldn't remember seeing the horse in the Devines' stable.

"Oh, he's not ours," Kate replied. "You don't think a horse of ours would be that cattle-shy, do you?"

Carole shook her head. "Of course not. That's why I was wondering." All the horses on the Bar None were familiar with cattle, even if they weren't cutting horses.

"The horse is a movie star, just like Skye," Kate explained.

"You've got to be kidding! You mean they brought their own horse?" Carole asked, incredulous.

"All the way from Beverly Hills," Kate said. "He's called Sir Prize. He was in a very popular little kids' movie last year, and the producers specifically wanted Skye to ride him in *Cowboy Come Home*."

Carole was flabbergasted. She had never heard of anything so stupid. They could have had their pick of experienced ranch horses, and instead they had flown in a pretty face. "That horse has probably never seen a cow in his life," Carole murmured.

Kate's response came quickly. "No kidding," she said drily. "But, hey, that's Hollywood."

36

THE NEXT MORNING the girls were up at dawn to enjoy the hearty ranch breakfast that Kate's mother, Phyllis, had prepared. The Devines were busy serving the crew breakfast outside, so The Saddle Club had the kitchen table to themselves. Over eggs, bacon, and toast, they discussed Skye's problems.

"The problem is that Skye doesn't have any real problems," Carole said. "He's not a champion, but he's riding well. There are two reasons why the scene isn't working: the director and Skye's horse."

Stevie reached for the platter of eggs and served herself

a second helping. "Everyone can just sit back and relax because I have the perfect solution," she said between bites.

Lisa and Carole eyed her skeptically. Somehow Stevie's "perfect solutions" had a way of being more complicated than the problems themselves. "All right. Get it over with. What's the solution?" Lisa asked resignedly.

Stevie pretended to be shocked. "Such doubt, Lisa! And from a friend? I can hardly believe it!"

"Stevie," Carole warned.

Stevie took her time buttering her third piece of toast. Then, sensing that her friends' patience had reached its limit, she revealed her one-word solution to all Skye's problems: "Stewball."

"Stewball?" Carole asked.

Stevie nodded.

"Stewball the horse?" Lisa asked.

"Yes! Of *course* Stewball the horse. If Skye rides him in the movie, all his problems will be solved. Stewball is the perfect cutting horse. He could make a stark beginner look like a champion cowboy."

"But Stevie, you heard what Kate said. Sir Prize isn't just any horse. He's famous. The director's not going to want to replace him after flying him out here to be in the movie," Lisa said.

"He will when he sees Stewball," Stevie predicted confidently.

"But he doesn't know the first thing about horses," Lisa reminded her. "How are we going to convince him that Stewball is better than Sir Prize?"

"We'll have him watch Stewball in action. Even a total idiot could see the difference between those two horses," Stevie said.

"I don't know . . . ," Lisa said.

Stevie set her fork down with a clatter. "Where's the Saddle Club spirit? It's worth a try, isn't it? You two aren't getting intimidated by a little old Hollywood director, are you? Stewball is our best shot!"

Lisa and Carole were doubtful, but they had to admit that Stevie had a point. Stewball's skill was just what Skye needed to look convincing in the cutting scenes. "The worst the director can do is say no," Carole said.

"Maybe he's not as dumb as we think," Lisa commented. "Maybe he will be able to understand that Stewball is the better man for the job—er, horse for the part."

As they finished breakfast and cleared the table, the girls worked out the details. Stevie wanted to speak to the director right away—the sooner they could persuade him, the better. "I say we go out and get Stewball ready now.

We bring him over to the director's trailer and surprise him with the idea. We'll say, 'This is the best cutting horse in the West and he ought to be in your movie.' Then I'll do an on-the-spot demonstration just to give the director a hint of what a great horse Stewball is. After a lesson or two, Skye can ride him in the cutting scene. It will be so perfect that the director won't care one bit about firing Sir Prize and hiring Stewball."

Won over by Stevie's enthusiasm, Carole and Lisa followed her out to the barn. They cross tied Stewball and set about giving him a real Saddle Club once-over. Stevie started with a currycomb, Lisa with a hoof pick, and Carole with a mane-and-tail comb. Stewball craned his neck to watch them.

"He's saying, 'What's all the fuss, guys?'" Stevie translated. "I'll bet he's never had this much attention in his life."

"That's because he's a real working horse," said Carole. "He does his job, and he doesn't expect to be fussed over."

"Unlike Sir Prize. That horse probably has a whole army of grooms," Lisa said dryly.

"But I'd take Stewball over Sir Prize any day of the week. And you know it, don't you, boy?" Stevie asked. She felt in her pockets for the pieces of carrot she had filched from the Devines' kitchen.

40

In response Stewball raised his head, pricked his ears up, and eyed her curiously. Stevie laughed out loud. Stewball always looked slightly comical, with his chestnut-and-white patchwork face and his splashy pinto coat. Now his expression highlighted his funny appearance. "Yes, I do have a carrot for you. Imagine that," Stevie told him. After she fed him the treat, she gave him a big hug. Stewball immediately laid his ears back.

"He doesn't go for that mushy stuff, Stevie," Lisa said, giggling.

"I know," Stevie said with a sigh. "I guess I'm feeling overprotective today. I've never been a stage mother before, you know."

"Imagine how Skye's mother must have felt before he auditioned for the first time," Carole mused, picking up a body brush.

"You think Skye *has* a mother?" Stevie asked.

Lisa looked at Stevie as if she were a creature from outer space. "Of course he has a mother!" she said.

"I'm kidding! It just seems strange that a movie star like Skye was ever a normal, unfamous kid with a normal mother who made him wash behind his ears and put Band-Aids on his cuts and stuff, doesn't it?" said Stevie.

Carole and Lisa thought for a minute. "I guess it does," Carole agreed. "But I think that's why Skye is such a nice person, even though he's famous. He probably has a very supportive family."

"And that's probably why he's so polite. His parents must have taught him good manners," Lisa said.

"Don't forget good-looking!" Stevie put in. "He had to get those 'cute' genes from somewhere."

As they brushed and rubbed Stewball's coat, the girls chatted more about Skye. They were extremely pleased that he was fitting in so well at the ranch and that Kate and her family genuinely liked him.

"He's such a great guy, it would be hard not to like him," Lisa concluded when Stevie went to get the tack. As she finished speaking and turned back to Stewball, a stall door at the end of the aisle swung open and John Brightstar emerged, wheeling a cart with a pitchfork in it. Lisa jumped at the noise, then felt her face turn red. Once again John had overheard her raving about Skye. It wasn't that she'd said anything wrong or untrue, but it made her feel awkward to know that John had probably listened to their whole conversation.

To cover up her embarrassment, Lisa greeted John enthusiastically. "Hey! What are you up to this morning?"

John paused with the cart. He looked tired and frustrated. "Hi, Lisa. I'm just finishing the mucking out. That was my last stall."

42

"If you're free now, do you want to come with us to introduce Stewball to the director? We're trying to get him a part in the movie," Lisa explained.

"Not just *a* part—*the* part. The lead role," said Stevie, returning from the tack room.

"Thanks, but I can't," John said, his voice heavy. "I still have to do the morning haying. We're way behind today. I spent two hours positioning horses in the corral for a 'candid' shot of the ranch."

"That doesn't sound fun," Lisa said glumly. Then she brightened. "Hey if you're so busy, why don't I help you instead?"

"But what about Stewball?" John asked.

"Stevie and Carole can take him over, right, guys?" Lisa asked. She didn't want to miss Stewball's introduction, but right then, helping John seemed more important.

Stevie and Carole agreed. "Absolutely. If you finish, come meet us over there," Stevie suggested.

John seemed genuinely pleased by Lisa's offer. The two of them chatted companionably as they walked to the back of the barn and climbed the ladder to the hayloft. When he got to the top, John gave Lisa his hand and helped her up the last couple of rungs.

"This will be great," John said. "With two people we can finish in—"

43

In the middle of his sentence, John stopped. A look of astonishment and then of anger crossed his face. With a quick look around, Lisa saw what had upset him. The loft, which normally held more than a hundred bales of hay, was empty.

"What happened to the hay?" Lisa asked.

"I know exactly what happened," John said furiously. "I just can't believe it. Last night the set designer came to speak to my dad about getting some hay to use in one of the scenes. Dad had me show the guy out here to the loft. We figured he meant five or ten bales!"

"But he took it all?" Lisa asked with a gulp.

"He sure did! Cleaned us right out! Wouldn't you think he'd realize that the horses need it?" John cried.

Lisa didn't know how to respond. John had every right to be angry. It would take him the better part of the morning to clear up this latest Hollywood mess. "What are you going to do?" she asked quietly.

John shrugged, his expression grim. "I'll have to talk to my father," he said. He focused briefly on Lisa, and his face softened. "Look, I'll handle it. You go help Carole and Stevie with Stewball. They'll be glad to have you with them," he said.

After a minute, Lisa agreed. She knew that she couldn't do anything more to help John. As she left the loft, she offered to mention the missing hay to Skye if she saw him.

"Skye Ransom?" John said, his voice full of disdain. "Come on! The big star isn't going to take time out to deal with a problem like this."

"You've got Skye all wrong," Lisa retorted. "He *would* care about this. He's not some stuck-up celebrity!" Without giving John a chance to reply, Lisa hurried down the ladder. She didn't want to hear John's response. In fact, she didn't want to see any more of this side of him. Period.

Running hard, Lisa caught up with Carole and Stevie on their way over. "That was fast!" Carole said.

"We didn't get to do the haying after all," Lisa said.

"Why not?" Stevie asked.

"Because Hollywood got to the hayloft first," said Lisa.

"Huh?" Stevie said.

"I'll tell you later. For now we have to concentrate on Stewball," Lisa said. Things with John were so confusing at the moment that she wanted to wait to talk to her friends until she could explain everything in detail.

"He looks good, doesn't he?" Steve asked.

"He's shining—at least to the extent that a skewbald can shine," Lisa assured her. Because pintos had so much white in their coats, they didn't glow the same way a bay or a chestnut did.

45

"What's the difference between a skewbald and a pie-bald, anyway?" Stevie asked. "I've never really known the difference, even though I know Stewball's a skewbald."

Carole spoke up promptly. "A piebald has large, irregular patches of white and black. A skewbald has large, irregular patches of white and any other color except black. Do you know an easy way to remember?" When Stevie and Lisa shook their heads, Carole continued, "Just remember this: 'Four-and-twenty *black*birds baked in a *pie*.' And, Stevie, I think skewbald Stewball looks stupendous."

"At least he's not nervous. Stage fright can ruin even the best performers," Lisa remarked. Lisa knew all about nerves and auditions. She had starred in the Willow Creek Players' production of *Annie*.

"Yup, I'd say he's cool as a cucumber," Carole agreed.

"You mean, as a carrot," Stevie joked.

The girls kidded one another until they reached the line of trailers that were temporary homes for the cast and crew. It took only a few minutes for Stevie to locate the door marked BLAKE PRATT, DIRECTOR. She handed Stewball's reins to Carole and rapped on the door. Almost immediately the door opened and she was ushered inside. Lisa and Carole waited nervously for her to reappear. They knew that Stevie had superhuman powers of persuasion,

46

but from what they had seen of Blake Pratt, Director, he was a force to be reckoned with.

A few minutes later, Stevie burst through the door. "It's settled! He's coming right out! He said he never misses a chance to see new talent. He'll only give us five minutes now, but I said that was fine. Give me a leg up, will you?"

Patting Stevie on the back, Lisa put ten fingers together and boosted her into the saddle.

"Good luck!" Carole whispered.

The trailer door opened again, and the director stepped out. He put a hand up to shield his eyes from the bright Western sun—and burst into hysterical laughter. "Ha, ha, ha! Very funny! You want me to put *that* in a movie? Good joke!" He turned around and called for his wife. "Honey, you gotta come see this! Funniest-looking horse I ever saw! Everybody, get a load of this!"

Lisa and Carole stood rooted to their positions. Stevie sat motionless on Stewball. It was worse than a bad nightmare. It was totally horrifying, and it was really happening. One by one the trailers' inhabitants poked their heads out or came outside. In a matter of minutes dozens of people were screeching with laughter and pointing at poor skewbald Stewball.

"She wanted Skye to ride *that* in the movie!" the director screamed, doubling over at his own joke.

47

"This might be embarrassing to us, but it's downright insulting to Stewball," Carole whispered to Lisa. The girls looked over at the horse, whose ears were twitching as he listened to the director's braying laugh.

There was only one person aside from The Saddle Club who wasn't laughing. Skye stepped forward from the crowd. "I wish I *could* ride this horse in the movie," he said defiantly. "He's the best cutting horse for hundreds of miles. Unfortunately, *some* people know a lot more about 'lights, camera, action' than they do about horses!"

Skye's words fell on deaf ears. The director was already walking off, still laughing loudly.

AFTER THE MORNING'S fiasco, lunch was a glum affair. Carole tried to be optimistic: At least they could still use Stewball to help train Skye. They were going to give him a lesson that afternoon. But it was going to be touch and go trying to get him ready within a couple of days.

They all felt terrible that they'd exposed Stewball to such humiliation. He was a smart, sensitive horse, and, walking back to the barn, he had looked downcast, as if he had understood that the crowd had been making fun of him.

In an attempt to cheer them up, Mrs. Devine brought out a tub of ice cream for dessert. "Help yourselves, girls, and try to remember that it's better to face any problem with enthushiasm," she advised. "I have to pick Kate up in town, so we'll see you at dinner." She left the ice cream on the table and headed out.

The Saddle Club decided to follow Kate's mother's advice and perk up. They ate their fill, washed their plates, and walked back out to the stable to get Stewball ready for his lesson with Skye.

"Hey, you know what?" Carole said suddenly. "I just had an idea. Why don't I go and work with Sir Prize while you two teach Skye. I can find out how much he knows and doesn't know, and that way we can separate which problems are his and which are Skye's."

Lisa and Stevie thought Carole's plan was excellent. Both of them knew that any horse—and particularly any horse as poorly trained as Sir Prize seemed to be—would benefit from a schooling session with Carole. They parted ways at the barn. Sir Prize was not stabled in the main barn but had private quarters in the Devines' stallion barn, which had been cleared just for his stay.

"I hope His Royal Movie-Star Highness is in his dressing room. Otherwise, I'll have to chase him down," said Carole.

"Don't you mean His Royal *Horse*ness?" Stevie asked.
Carole made a gagging expression and went on her way.

SKYE'S LESSON WENT better than the girls had dared hope.
First they had him ride Stewball around the ring, but that
got boring, and Skye was eager to try some cattle work.
There were a few steers corralled near the ring. Lisa suggested that Skye work on singling one out of the "herd,"
the way he would have to in the movie.

"Here goes nothing!" Skye called as he entered the
corral and shut the gate behind him.

Leaning over the fence, the girls gave him the thumbs-
up sign.

Stevie's predictions were right. At first Skye tried to
control Stewball. When Stewball stopped to size up the
cattle, Skye urged him closer to the steers. Stewball dug
his hooves in.

"Come on, Stewball, don't act up," Skye urged, using
his legs to try to move the horse forward. Stewball laid his
ears back and ignored his rider. One of the steers, made
restless by the interruption, moved away from the others,
looking as if he might bolt to the other end of the corral.
Stewball was on him in a flash. He sidestepped, he turned,
he stepped forward to intimidate the steer and back to
cover him. Finally he stopped and stood stock-still.

51

"Throw your lasso!" Lisa yelled, and Skye threw, whirling the rope above his head, then letting it fly through the air and around the steer's neck.

"Yippee!" Skye yelled. He was so thrilled with his performance that Stevie and Lisa had to beg him to let the steer go so that he could try again. "But what if I don't make it this time?" Skye called anxiously.

"Please, Skye!" Stevie answered. "This is *Stewball* you're riding. Have a little faith!"

During the rest of the lesson, Skye learned to sit back and let Stewball do the work. Like most Stewball beginners, Skye's instinct was to try to think for the horse, but Lisa and Stevie coached him into pretending Stewball was an easy chair.

"So all I have to do is sit here and look good?" Skye asked the girls.

"Right. And swing your rope. We haven't managed to teach Stewball to use a lasso yet," Stevie replied.

Skye hopped off and patted Stewball as if he'd never stop. It was the most enthusiastic the girls had ever seen him about a horse. Once they had considered making Skye an honorary Saddle Club member, but they had realized that Skye wasn't truly horse-crazy. Nobody would have believed it, though, listening to him singing Stewball's praises now.

When Skye had exclaimed "This horse is incredible!" for the millionth time, Lisa cut him off, saying, "You're not so bad yourself, Skye. You've really done your homework for this part."

Skye grinned sheepishly. "I guess I learned my lesson after *City Cowboy*," he said.

Lisa and Stevie smiled, remembering the movie Skye had been filming when they had met him.

"Luckily," Skye concluded, putting his arm around Lisa and giving her shoulder a friendly squeeze, "Lisa Atwood came to the rescue."

Lisa grinned, looked up, and stopped dead in her tracks. She was face-to-face with John! For a few seconds she was speechless. She couldn't believe it: Whenever she looked or sounded friendly with Skye, John would appear. It was so ridiculous Lisa would have laughed—except that the hurt, angry expression on John's face stopped her. What made it worse was that, because of the morning's disappointment, Lisa had completely forgotten to mention the missing hay to Skye.

"Did you—did you find the hay, John?" Lisa asked tentatively, extracting herself from under Skye's arm.

"Yes, we got enough of it back to do the morning feeding, and Dad ordered another shipment," John replied.

Lisa couldn't tell if he was still annoyed. While she was

trying to think of something to add, Skye spoke up. "I don't think we've met. I'm Skye Ransom," he said, extending his hand.

John took it but didn't meet Skye's eyes. "John Brightstar," he muttered.

"Do you work on the ranch?" Skye inquired.

John nodded but didn't say anything.

"Do you ride, too?" Skye asked.

John smirked. "It's pretty hard to grow up on a ranch and not learn how to ride," he said.

Skye looked embarrassed. "Of course—I should have known you would ride."

Even though John was being rude, Lisa felt she should be loyal to him in front of Skye. "John is an excellent rider," she said. "He's training his own horse, Tex."

"Wow, that's great," Skye said. "I'd love to have a horse to train."

"Would you really?" John said sarcastically.

"Yes, I think it would be fun," Skye answered.

"It's a lot more than fun," John retorted. "It's hard work. But then, you might not know the meaning of those words, since you're a famous movie star."

Before Skye could answer, John turned on his heel and stalked off.

"Boy, something's eating him, huh?" Skye said.

Lisa felt her face flush. She was angry and embarrassed—angry at John for embarrassing her in front of Skye. Stevie came to the rescue. "Come on, we'd better get Stewball back for his rubdown. He's had a long day," she said.

Lisa nodded, recovering herself. "He sure has. But I think the afternoon did him good. If I've ever seen a horse look depressed, Stewball did this morning."

Skye shook his head in disgust. "I wish I could have Blake Pratt fired, after the way he acted. Unfortunately, he's the one who could fire me. If this part didn't mean so much to my career, I swear I'd walk off the job.

"At least I've got Stewball to train me now," Skye went on. "I'm sure I'll be able to teach Sir Prize everything I'm learning in no time."

Lisa and Stevie exchanged glances. Neither of them had the heart to tell Skye that it could take years to train a good cutting horse—and that the horse needed to have the right personality, which Sir Prize didn't. Having Skye do so well on Stewball was wonderful and disappointing at the same time. It just proved what Stevie had known all along: that if Skye could ride Stewball in the movie, all his problems would be solved. Instead, they were only beginning.

Skye saved the girls from having to say anything in

response. He was due at a cast meeting for a run-through of a scene. Thanking them and patting Stewball again, he left them at the entrance to the main barn.

As Lisa and Stevie led Stewball inside, Carole joined them. She was red-faced and panting and looked ready to explode.

"What happened? Didn't the lesson go well?" Lisa asked. It wasn't like Carole to get so worked up.

"It hardly went at all!" Carole exclaimed. "The so-called animal trainer wouldn't let me take her precious property out of his stall until I signed about nine release forms! And even then, he had to wear every kind of boot, bandage, and pad ever invented. Once I got on, it went from terrible to horrible! That horse doesn't know the first thing about Western aids. He doesn't even neck-rein properly. I got so upset comparing him to Stewball that finally I had to quit. I was getting nowhere fast."

Stevie and Lisa felt their hearts sink. Carole's news was grim. They had been entertaining a faint hope that maybe Sir Prize just needed a good rider to set him straight. Clearly, that was far from the case. Carole had worked with all kinds of ornery, disobedient, green, and sluggish horses, and she almost never lost her cool. Like any good rider, she understood that training required infinite pa-

56

tience. But this situation was evidently more than she could handle.

"There's a solution to our problems somewhere," Stevie said. "There always is. We've just got to put our heads together and think." She knew that it was crucial for them to stay optimistic. If they gave up now, Skye would have no hope of riding in the movie, and they would have failed him, not only as technical advisers, but also as friends. "If only Stewball could talk. He'd tell us what to do," she said wistfully.

6

"COULD YOU PASS the salt, Lisa? Lisa? Hello-o, Earth to Lisa." Stevie waved her hands, and Lisa finally snapped to attention.

"Oh, sorry, I didn't hear you. What did you want? The sugar?" Lisa asked.

Stevie smiled tolerantly. "No, the salt," she said gently, resisting the impulse to tease her.

Lisa had been distracted all through dinner. She hadn't taken part in any of the conversations. Now she was staring at her plate, pushing her rice and beans around with her fork. Stevie had a pretty good idea why. The confrontation between John and Skye had been ugly. John hadn't acted like himself at all. In fact, he was the one who had *made* it a confrontation when it should have been a friendly introduction. Poor Lisa had been caught in the middle.

Back in the bunkhouse, Stevie questioned Lisa directly. "Is it what I think?" she asked.

Lisa nodded. "If you mean John, yes," she replied.

"Tell Carole what happened," Stevie suggested.

Lisa recounted the story, going back to the scene in the hayloft, where John had said that Skye wouldn't care about the missing hay. "I can see why he's annoyed about all the extra work and the attitude of most of the Hollywood people, but why does he have to group Skye with the rest of them?" she asked.

"I have one word," Stevie said dramatically. *"Jealousy."*

"That's what I was going to say," Carole said.

"I did think of that," Lisa admitted. "Practically every time John sees me I'm saying what a great guy Skye is."

"Exactly," Stevie said.

"But it's true!" Lisa protested. "Skye *is* a great guy. And so is John. I'm not going to pretend to John that I don't like Skye!"

"Too bad. Then it could really get interesting," Stevie said, a wicked glint in her eye.

Carole threw a pillow at her. "Some friend you are!"

"Just kidding," Stevie said. Then she added impishly, "Maybe you should pretend that you do like Skye. I mean *like* like him, you know? To make John even more jealous! Then John would confront Skye and they could fight over you." Stevie's hazel eyes lit up at the thought of so much scheming.

"Don't listen to a word she says, Lisa!" Carole said, glaring at Stevie. "Honesty is the best policy. You should tell John how you feel—that you and Skye are just friends and that John had better stop acting like such a baby about it. Then the air will be cleared and you and John can go on the way you did before."

"I keep meaning to say something to him, but we haven't been able to spend any time together," Lisa explained.

"Well, there's no time like the present," Stevie said brightly.

"You mean now?" Lisa asked. The three of them had already brushed their teeth and changed into their pajamas.

Stevie nodded. "I'll bet if you went out to the barn right now you could catch John finishing up out there."

60

"She does have a point," Carole agreed.

Lisa thought for a minute. Stevie was probably right. She knew that John had the habit of going out to the barn in the evenings even if he didn't have work to do. And with the extra duties the movie had brought, there was a good chance he had gone back after his dinner to finish a few barn chores. The more she thought about the idea, the less crazy it seemed. "All right, I'll do it! I'll go out and talk to him right now," she announced.

Stevie and Carole helped her into her bathrobe and barn shoes and promised to stay up until she got back. Then they packed her out the door, wishing her luck.

Lisa stepped out into the night air. It was a clear evening, and the sky was lit up with stars. Lisa always noticed the difference between the sky at the Bar None and the sky at home in Virginia. Somehow out West it seemed larger—and the stars seemed brighter. Even with the ranch buildings and the Hollywood trailers nearby, the land felt vast and empty. Breathing the clear, sharp air, Lisa thought she understood why some people could never leave the West. John was one of them. His ancestors had lived in the Western states for centuries—before the states were even states. She knew that he loved the land as if it were a person. That might have been one of the reasons the Hollywood invasion had upset him so much.

Shivering a little, Lisa hurried toward the light in the stable.

Inside, John was wearily raking the dirt aisle so that it would be neat for the morning. Lisa hated to disturb him in his work, but she knew that if she didn't, it would be impossible to talk to him anytime soon. "John?"

John looked up and smiled—his old, warm smile—when he saw her. "What are you doing out here?" he asked.

"I came to say hi. We all sort of figured you'd still be out here," she said.

John let out a long breath. "You got that right. I grabbed a bite at home and then came back."

"Do you want some help?" Lisa asked.

"Sure. That would be great. There's another rake just inside the door there."

Lisa took the rake, and they worked without speaking for several minutes. She didn't want to break the companionable silence, and suddenly she had cold feet about bringing up Skye. She was glad when John spoke first.

"It's nice out here at night, isn't it?" he said.

"Yes, it's great," Lisa agreed. "It's so quiet and peaceful."

They came to the end of the aisle and stood leaning on their rakes. "I used to sleep in the barn all the time when I was little," John said. "I'd always find some excuse—some horse that had a cold or a foal that needed watching. Dad was pretty nice about pretending that whatever I thought up was important enough for me to be here. . . ." John's voice drifted off as he lost himself in the memory.

"Well," Lisa said, chuckling, "if you need an excuse now, I'm sure Sir Prize could use another twenty-four-hour guardian."

The minute Lisa made the joke, she was sorry. John's face changed from content to frustrated in a matter of seconds. "The way they treat that horse is ridiculous!" he said. "Not to mention flying him in to the ranch in the first place."

"I know. We think so, too," Lisa said, relieved that the two of them could agree on something to do with the movie. "And he's barely even trained. Carole was riding him this afternoon and she couldn't get him to do anything."

"Why was Carole riding him?" John asked.

Lisa bit her lip. She'd come this far, though—she couldn't stop now. "She's helping get him ready for Skye to ride in the movie. We're all helping Skye get ready. That's why Stevie and I were giving him a lesson on Stewball this afternoon."

"I *had* noticed that you've been spending all your time

63

with him," John said pointedly, pressing his lips into a tight line.

Lisa clenched her hands in annoyance. "Why shouldn't we? We're his technical advisers for the movie. Not to mention his friends," she said. She tried to keep her voice calm, but she could hear it quavering.

"His *best* friends, from what I can tell," John shot back.

"Skye has a lot of friends," Lisa said hotly. "He's a friendly person—which you would have noticed this afternoon if you hadn't been so bent on insulting him."

"That Hollywood pretty boy could use a couple of insults to take him down a peg or two!" John retorted.

"He's not stuck-up!" Lisa said. "You just think he is because the other Hollywood people are."

"Well, I can tell you one way he's like the others: He's an idiot! He asked *me* if I knew how to ride! What does he think I am, some kind of servant who's not allowed to go near the horses?"

Lisa stared at John, astonished by his outburst. She knew that if he could have heard himself, he would have understood how ridiculous he sounded. But he was so upset that he was saying whatever came into his mind. "Skye was just being polite this afternoon," she said finally.

John didn't respond. Instead he began to rerake the aisle. Lisa watched him attack the dirt for a minute or two. Reasoning with him was clearly not going to work tonight. But if it didn't work tonight, she wondered, when would it?

BACK IN THE BUNKHOUSE, Lisa hardly had to say anything to Carole and Stevie. One look at her deflated expression and they guessed how the conversation had gone. "The plan backfired?" Stevie asked, gesturing for Lisa to climb up and join them in Carole's bunk.

Lisa nodded. "Instead of telling John that Skye is only a friend, I ended up defending Skye again." She swung up into the bunk.

"It's too bad that John doesn't know Skye. If he could get to know him, he'd realize that Skye is a good guy," Carole mused.

"But they're both too busy. Skye's trying to get ready for the final shoot, John has tons of extra work—how are we supposed to find the time for them to hang out?" Lisa asked. After the movie crew left, things could go back to normal. But by then, The Saddle Club would be back in Willow Creek, and Lisa's friendship with John might be beyond repairing.

"I know!" Stevie exclaimed.

"Let me guess. You have just one word to say," said Carole.

"Nope, sorry: two," Stevie said. *"Technical advisers."*

"Huh?" said Carole and Lisa in unison.

"Why don't we ask John to join the team?" said Stevie.

"But he hates Hollywood and he thinks Skye is an idiot. Why would he want to help out?" Lisa asked.

"Maybe he hates Hollywood because he's not involved. He's stuck doing all the hard work while everyone else has a glamorous job. And we know the reason he doesn't like Skye is that he doesn't know him. If he worked with us, it might solve both problems," Stevie reasoned.

"If we could convince him somehow," Lisa said.

"Oh, convincing him will be easy," said Stevie. "We'll just make it boss's orders. I'll bet if we speak to Frank Devine and explain the situation, he can order John to be part of the team."

Carole raised her eyebrows doubtfully. "You mean Lisa is supposed to tell Frank Devine that John Brightstar thinks she has a crush on Skye Ransom, so we need him on the technical advisory team?"

"Not exactly," said Stevie. "We'll have to edit the story somehow—rearrange it, change a few details, recast the leading lady—"

66

"—cut to the chase, change the makeup—Stevie, I think you've been hanging out with Blake Pratt too long!" Carole kidded.

Stevie grinned. "When in Rome, do as the Romans do," she said.

"So, when on a movie set, do as the Los Angelenos do?" Carole said suspiciously.

Lisa sighed. "All I can say is that I'm glad Stevie's directing this scene."

7

THE NEXT MORNING Stevie got up earlier than usual. Before breakfast, she went to the Devines', where she found Frank Devine glancing at the morning paper. "Any good news this morning?" she inquired.

Frank held out the front section for her to see. "Yes, there is: the weather. The rain's supposed to hold off for another day. I was hoping it would hold off until these people pack out of here, but that's probably wishful thinking. If everyone and everything gets drenched, it's going to be even more work for the staff."

Stevie saw her opportunity and seized it. "Speaking of more work . . ."

"Yes, Stevie?" Frank asked.

"We all think there's one person on your staff who's working harder than anybody else," Stevie said.

Frank didn't look surprised by the comment. "I don't have to ask who that is," he said. "I can't get John to leave the stables at night, and he's out there at dawn. Then he spends the whole day doing Hollywood chores . . . well, we all do that, but somehow he'll never quit. It's as if he's trying to prove something to someone."

Frank's words gave Stevie a sudden insight. Of course! Part of the reason John was working so hard was probably to impress Lisa. He wouldn't have admitted it, but it was true. But instead of being impressed, Lisa felt bad that the movie was taking up so much of his time.

"So, what do you suggest I do to give the boy a break?" Frank asked.

"We've got the perfect solution. We really need him on the technical advisory team. There are more problems with the horses than we expected, and John would be a huge help," said Stevie.

"He sure would. If he can't solve a horse problem, I don't know who can," Frank responded.

"So, can we have him?" Stevie asked eagerly.

"You'll get no objection from me," Frank answered. "I'm more than happy to let him go for a couple of hours a day. It will be good for him to be with you girls and enjoy himself. He's been working much too hard. Tell him I said it's an order, all right? Now, what do you say we get some oatmeal while it's hot?"

"You'll get no objection from me," Stevie said.

AFTER BREAKFAST AND Stevie's thumbs-up report, Lisa approached John. She found him in the feed room dumping sacks of grain into the trash cans where it was stored. She was a little nervous about how he would react after what had happened the night before, but John was apologetic and seemed embarrassed about their argument. "You mean we help out whoever needs it?" he asked, when she had finished describing their job.

Lisa nodded. "Right. Anyone who needs horse-related help, that is." She specifically didn't bring up Skye. John could find out later who needed their help most.

"Okay, count me in," John said.

"Great, then come on. We're all going to watch the morning shoot," Lisa said.

John hesitated a minute, looking around the room.

70

Then he gathered up the empty grain sacks and stacked them neatly by the door. "All right. Why not? One of the other hands can take over from here."

"Even Frank Devine thinks you're working too hard," Lisa told him shyly, as they left the barn. "He said to order you to come have fun with us." Lisa hadn't been surprised to hear that John had been putting in more hours than any other employee. He had such a strong sense of responsibility that he would do whatever jobs needed doing instead of finding someone else to share the work. Lisa had been more like that herself before meeting Stevie and Carole. Through them, she had learned that it was pointless to tackle huge projects alone. Now she willingly enlisted their help in almost everything she did.

John and Lisa met Stevie and Carole on the viewing platform where they had sat before. This time none of them had trouble getting past the security guards. "I think they've noticed that we have friends in high places," Stevie remarked, with a nod in Skye's direction.

"Yeah, you can't get much higher than the *Skye*, can you?" John teased.

Lisa did a double take. Had she heard correctly? John? Making a joke about Skye? Maybe some of what she'd said the night before had sunk in. Maybe John realized how

71

badly he'd been behaving. Before she could wonder about it more, someone on the set screamed, "Quiet!" The filming had begun.

At first it was exciting. Blake Pratt, Director, was truly in his element: barking orders left and right; doing retakes; screaming "Makeup!" when Skye needed a touch-up; and generally keeping things rolling. But even in this new scene, without the horse and cattle, it was next to impossible to get a perfect take. Skye was having a lot of trouble following the director's orders. And as interesting as the whole process was, after watching Skye get out of a pickup truck, slam the door, whistle for his dog, and push his cowboy hat back on his head seventeen times, even his biggest fans, The Saddle Club, were getting a little fidgety.

The dog was evidently bored, too. On the eighteenth take, instead of coming when Skye whistled, he began to yap and run in circles. Then he ran pell-mell for the director, growling and snapping. Blake Pratt was not a man to take the dog's antics in stride. As John and The Saddle Club watched, he exploded into a rage. "Get that thing outta here!" he screamed. "Get it away from me! You shut your trap, you stupid cur! Scram! I said now!"

Stevie leaned in toward her friends. "This guy isn't

72

exactly the world's biggest animal lover, is he?" she whispered.

By this point the dog had the director backed up against the viewing platform. The crew, stifling laughter, had made no move to rescue their boss.

"I guess everyone wishes they could be the dog," Lisa said, "and finally give him a piece of their mind."

Finally, when it was clear that nobody was going to do anything, John stood up. He walked to the edge of the platform and spoke to the dog in a low, firm voice. The dog cocked his ears and sat back on his haunches, listening. John told him to lie down, which he did, his tail wagging.

Now that he was safe, Blake Pratt started sputtering with anger. He turned on John, who had come down and was holding the dog. "You idiot! Why didn't you come get him sooner? I could have been killed by that rabid hellhound! One bite from him and I'd be dead! You hear me? Dead! What were you thinking? Why, I oughta—!" Shaking his fists at John, the little man stomped off.

A member of the crew yelled, "Fifteen-minute break for coffee!" and The Saddle Club scrambled down to join John.

"What a jerk!" Stevie cried. "Here you were, trying to help!"

"Listen," John said quickly, "I'd better get back to the stables. I've already been away for over an hour. Make sure you get this dog to the animal trainer, okay?" Before the girls could think of a way to urge him not to go, John had slipped into the crowd.

"Hey! Wait a minute!" Skye called, running up to join them.

Seeing him approach, Lisa understood why John had run off. Even if Skye wanted to thank him, it would have made John feel awkward after he had been so rude the day before.

"Where did John go?" Skye asked. "I wanted to tell him how much we appreciated his stepping in like that."

Carole began, "We don't know, but we—"

"He had some important errands to run for the Devines," Lisa said firmly.

"Oh. Well, if you see him, tell him thanks for me, okay? As you could see, everybody on the crew was paralyzed. I think we all secretly hoped Rex would take a chunk out of Blake's leg," Skye admitted.

Silently Lisa was thankful that Skye still seemed willing to be friendly with John. Being in the movie business, Skye was probably used to dealing with rudeness. Evidently it didn't ruffle his feathers.

74

"So, Skye, exactly how many more times are you going to have to shoot this scene?" Stevie asked.

Skye chuckled. "Sorry about that. It's not usually quite this boring," he said. "You see, this is a close-up shot, so we have to get everything perfect. If I twitch or squint too much or get hair in my face or *anything*, it shows. Other scenes—like, say, the scenes on horseback—are more distant: You'll see a horse and a rider, but the camera won't pick up every last blink." With a sigh, he added, "That's why they can use a double for my riding scenes."

"So the director's still talking about calling in a stuntman?" Lisa inquired.

Skye nodded gloomily. "Yes. He told me he wanted to make a few phone calls and fly somebody in today or tomorrow. He says we have to get one of the riding scenes done tomorrow afternoon, at three P.M. sharp. I told him that I think Sir Prize will be ready, and I also told him not to call anyone—not yet, anyway. But you can't trust Blake. He'll do anything when my back is turned," said Skye.

Although she had winced at Skye's mention of Sir Prize, Stevie said confidently, "Don't worry, Skye. The next time Blake sees you, you will be ready."

There was a longish pause before Carole and Lisa

jumped in to second Stevie's prediction. "Sure, Skye," said Carole. "Stevie's right."

"We wouldn't let you down," Lisa added.

Nearby, a voice barked over a bullhorn. "Skye Ransom. You're wanted in makeup. Ransom to makeup."

Skye seemed glad for the interruption. It obviously made him nervous to talk about the problem. "As they say in Hollywood, there's my cue," he said. "I'll see you this afternoon for the lesson."

When he had gone, The Saddle Club turned and fled the premises.

"Why the heck did I have to go and say that?" Stevie wailed.

"Why the heck did I have to agree with you?" Lisa groaned.

"Who cares? What I want to know is *how* the heck we're going to solve this one!" Carole said.

There was no question about it: The Saddle Club was panicked. Stevie called an emergency meeting in the tack room of the barn. On the way there, they met Kate coming from the trailers. They waved her over.

"Wait till you hear the latest!" Kate said, falling into step with them. "The spouses of the actors and film crew have decided that they're bored. So they asked my mother if we could arrange group trail rides for them, the way we

76

do for our usual guests! Isn't that too much? Mom and I have been working around the clock to keep them happy, we've hired extra help to provide maid service in the trailers, and now they want trail rides, too! I know they're paying a lot to use the place, but honestly, sometimes I'm not sure it's worth it."

Murmuring their sympathy, the girls insisted that Kate at least take time out to come to The Saddle Club meeting. She was eager to comply.

A few minutes later, after they had negotiated the maze of roped-off sections that lay between the set and the barn, the four of them were seated on the floor of the tack room. They filled Kate in on the grim outlook.

THE GIRLS TALKED about the problem for almost an hour, but they finally realized that all they could hope for was that Skye would somehow get lucky and pull off a couple of decent scenes with Sir Prize. "The most frustrating thing is that Skye isn't the real problem—the horse is. Skye might not be perfect, but with a good horse, he could do fine. And yet he's going to be the one who suffers if they call in a stuntman," Lisa pointed out.

"You're right. Sir Prize wouldn't care if his Hollywood career went down the tubes, would he?" Kate said.

Stevie giggled. "Maybe we should expose him to the

press! We could leak a story to the Beverly Hills gossip magazines that the great Sir Prize isn't much of a prize after all."

Everyone laughed, but Lisa remarked, "It's not as crazy as it sounds. Bad publicity can ruin a career. And in Hollywood, even animals have careers!"

The four girls wandered into the aisle of the barn. It was time to go get lunch so that they could be back to tack up Stewball for Skye's afternoon lesson. Carole cast an eye down the row of stalls, as she always did. What she saw at the end of the aisle made her start. The others followed her glance. There was a strange man nosing around the stalls. He was tall and blond. He looked a lot like Skye—same build, same hairstyle.

"Boy," Lisa murmured, "he could almost be Skye's"—she caught her breath—"Skye's double!"

8

BEFORE SKYE'S LESSON, Stevie, Lisa,.and Carole made a pact not to mention the double. Knowing that the man was actually on the premises would only worry Skye and make it hard for him to perform. With heavy hearts, they took Stewball to the corral to meet Skye. What chance did they have now that the stuntman had arrived? The director had clearly made up his mind that he didn't want Skye to ride. Still, they couldn't give up until the decision had been made. With Stevie setting the example, Carole and Lisa put on optimistic faces and went forward to greet Skye.

As it turned out, they needn't have bothered. The bad

news was written all over Skye's face. "Blake came clean to me after the shoot," he said. "He called the double last night. He said it makes him feel better knowing we have a sub. The guy is here right now, ready to take over whenever I give the word."

Stevie, Lisa, and Carole didn't know what to say. The situation had gone from bad to worse, and none of them could see how to change it. Now there was no reason to hide the fact that they had seen the stuntman on the property.

Skye barely reacted when they told him. "I figured we'd run into him soon," he said. "With the shoot scheduled for tomorrow, he's got nothing to do today but hang around and wait."

The girls nodded, trying to think of some comforting or encouraging words.

Often, when the chips were down, Stevie would give a rousing pep talk that would cheer everyone up. She had done it many times before. Usually she believed what she said. But sometimes, when The Saddle Club was in desperate straits, she would give the pep talk anyway—whether or not she believed in it. This was one of those times. Summoning all her creative powers, she started to speak.

"All right. Enough of this bad attitude! We can't throw

in the towel yet! It's three o'clock Tuesday. The tape rolls at three o'clock Wednesday. We all know what that means: We have twenty-four hours to figure something out. Twenty-four big, long hours. Right now we're going to give Skye his lesson on Stewball. We'll make it brief and then he'll switch to Sir Prize. Who knows, Skye, you might be right about Prize. He could surprise us all. But we can't quit now. You'll ride hard today, and we'll brainstorm hard tonight."

After a few more encouraging words, Stevie finished her speech. She surveyed the faces. Her friends didn't look completely convinced, but they did look a tiny bit more hopeful—especially Skye, who had thought all along that he could get Prize up to par for the scene. Enthusiasm, like pessimism, could be catching.

Carole volunteered to go saddle Prize. Stevie and Lisa gave Skye a leg up on Stewball and set to work. Their plan was to work on Skye's cutting skills some more. This time they had chosen a corral with several cows and older calves in it. Warming up outside the fence, Skye looked nervous and distracted. Like any horse, Stewball could tell, and he took advantage of Skye. He pretended to spook at leaves on the ground; he chucked his head up and down, playing with the bit; he broke from a jog to a lope and back to a jog.

His antics were just what Skye needed to make him concentrate. In a matter of minutes, Stevie and Lisa could tell that he had forgotten the next day's shoot, the movie, and his career and was thinking only about the horse underneath him.

"All right, let's get to it," Stevie ordered. "Why don't you try cutting that calf down there." She pointed to a large one in the middle of the group.

Skye entered the corral and shut the gate behind him. Then he let Stewball do the work. The calf was a feisty one. First he ducked farther into the herd; then he tried to take off down the corral. But Stewball moved more quickly than the calf did and got Skye into a perfect position. Skye and the calf faced off. The calf made a move to dart to one side, but Skye and Stewball turned to block him. The calf ducked the other way and was blocked again. The seconds ticked away as Skye and Stewball kept the calf from running to the rest of the herd. With a final, desperate effort, the calf got away and sprinted down the long side of the ring.

Watching from the sidelines, Lisa and Stevie burst into applause. They knew the victory was only a fleeting one, but it was a victory nonetheless. Right then, even small successes mattered a lot. They had to keep thinking positively.

"Nice job," said a low voice behind them.

To Lisa's delight, it was John. He'd been passing the corral and decided to watch for a minute or two. "John, I'm so glad you stopped by. Skye wants to thank you for taking care of the dog this morning," she said.

John smiled. "You mean the 'stupid cur'?" he joked. "Tell him it was nothing."

"No, really—" Lisa began to protest but stopped when she saw that John truly didn't want to be praised for what he had done. Instead she asked, "Can you stay and help us with the rest of the lesson?"

"Yeah, we'd love your input," Stevie said.

"No, I'd like to, but I really can't. With all this movie business, I haven't taken Tex out in days." John lowered his voice to a stage whisper. "I'm going to sneak in a quick ride."

"Great!" Lisa fairly shouted. It made her very happy that John had decided to take some time for himself. She also realized that John probably wasn't ready to jump right into their group: Whatever help he gave Skye would be on his own terms. "Tell Tex I say hi," Lisa added.

"I will," John promised, heading on his way. "And tell Skye to lower his stirrups a couple of holes. They're too high."

Stevie and Lisa turned to check.

"He's right," Lisa said.

"Yup. He's got them set more for Engish riding. I'll go tell him," said Stevie.

"Thanks, John," Lisa murmured toward his retreating back.

AFTER A HALF HOUR, Carole appeared with Sir Prize, and Skye switched horses. Stevie was sure that Stewball understood what was going on. As Skye mounted Prize, Stewball laid his ears back as if to sneer at him. "It's not my fault!" Skye complained. "Stevie, tell him not to look at me that way!"

"Sorry, Skye, but this horse holds a grudge for a long time," Stevie replied.

"Look, I'll make it up to you, okay, Stewball?" Skye said.

Stewball snorted loudly. Skye laughed. "He does belong in movies. He's the best actor I've seen in a while," he said. "That snort said more than most monologues."

The whole group headed toward another corral—an empty one. Even though time was crucial, they weren't about to start Prize with the cattle. First Skye had to show him who was boss.

Stevie and Lisa assumed that Carole would be eager to

impart what she'd learned from riding Prize the day before, but Carole said she needed to calm down first. Once
again, she had been a victim of the animal trainer's hyper-
active imagination. This time the woman had called
Frank Devine to check Carole's references so that she
could make sure Carole wasn't going to try to steal the
horse.

"Steal him!" Carole said, relating the story to the others. "You couldn't pay me to take him away!"

Skye said he was happy to warm up on his own. The
girls watched him putting the big, sluggish horse through
his paces. "The only time that horse perks up is when he's
around cattle," Carole commented. "And the only reason
he perks up then is that he wants to run away."

Carole let Stevie and Lisa help Skye for a few minutes
while she tried to get herself into a suitable mood for
teaching a lesson. Then she joined them in the corral.
She waved Skye over for a quick briefing. "First of all,
you're in charge, Skye, and Prize does what you want. No
ifs, ands, or buts—no ignoring your aids or pretending he
doesn't understand. This isn't a horse you have to baby.
This is a horse that needs a firm hand. He's used to getting
his way. Despite the fact that he's a movie star, I get the
feeling he's never had to perform in his life. He probably

just gets trotted around from place to place with little kids on his back. He's used to taking advantage of his rider. We're not going to let him. Got it?"

"Got it," Skye said, looking impressed.

When Carole went into her riding-instructor mode, she was a formidable presence. At Pony Club, where the more experienced riders taught the less experienced, she was a favorite with the younger kids. She always knew her stuff, and she explained it in a way they could understand. She wasn't like some instructors who got so caught up in little details that they couldn't see the big picture. Carole always saw the big picture and strived toward the ultimate goal: a horse and rider working together in harmony. Sometimes that took coaxing and quieting; sometimes it took firm discipline. But it always took patience, sensitivity, and a clear head.

And some days, Carole knew, an instructor had to be satisfied with progress in very small increments. Unfortunately, even though they all needed Sir Prize to transform himself instantly into the perfect cutting horse, today was one of those days. They had to start at the beginning, teaching Prize to neck-rein so that Skye could turn him on command. In spite of Stevie's pep talk, Skye's efforts, and her own enthusiasm, Carole found herself getting more and more doubtful.

86

Skye wasn't riding very well, either. Now that he'd had a chance to try a real cutting horse like Stewball, he was obviously frustrated by Prize's problems. "He's not listening to me, Carole, no matter what I do!" he complained after a particularly trying reining exercise. "He'll never be ready for tomorrow!"

"Take him out to the rail and start again," Carole said quietly. "This time I'll walk you through all the aids."

Stevie and Lisa had been hanging back, watching. Figuring she needed all the input she could get, Carole turned to beckon them to join her. She was surprised to see a third person leaning on the rail a few yards away from them. The blond, curly hair; the tall, slim build . . . "Of all the nerve!" Carole cried. Skye's stuntman had come to watch Skye ride. Too late, Carole realized that she shouldn't have said anything: Skye turned in the saddle and recognized his double at once.

"Don't pay any attention to him," Carole said, knowing that it would be next to impossible for Skye to follow her advice.

Skye squared his shoulders determinedly. "I won't, darn it. He can't get rid of me yet. I've still got today left to ride."

Out at the rail, Stevie and Lisa saw Skye notice the stuntman. They, of course, had seen him immediately but had kept quiet, hoping the double would go away. "I'm going to get rid of him," Stevie declared suddenly. "That's the least we can do for Skye." She walked over and greeted the man, making sure she didn't sound at all welcoming.

"Hello. How are you today?" the man asked politely.

"I'd be a whole lot better if you'd leave," Stevie said frankly, surprising even herself with how rude she could be.

"Would you now? Well, I'm sorry, I can't do that. Director's orders. I'm supposed to watch Skye like a hawk so's I can look like him as much as possible tomorrow," said the man.

"Look, I really think that if you left now, we'd all be—" Stevie stopped, thinking madly. Something had just occurred to her. Something very important. There was absolutely no reason on earth why the stuntman should leave. In fact, it would be good for him to *stay*—and see how awful Prize was. Even though the guy might be a more experienced rider than Skye, he couldn't be so much of a miracle worker that he wouldn't have trouble with Prize, too. Even Carole hadn't been able to get very far with the horse, and chances were, the stuntman wasn't as good as Carole. Maybe he wouldn't be able to do any better than Skye. Then the director would have to see how unfair he

88

was being. "Forget what I said: Make yourself at home. Watch all you want," Stevie said sweetly.

"Thank you, I will," the man replied.

Now that Stevie had had her important realization, she decided she might even be able to scare the double off if she hammed it up about how terrible Prize was. "You know this horse is barely trained?" she said.

"Yup, so I've heard through the grapevine."

"And he's scared of cattle."

"I heard that, too."

"I mean really scared. He tries to run when he sees them."

"Uh-huh." The man reached down and picked a blade of grass to chew on. He looked utterly unperturbed.

Stevie was so confused that she gave up beating around the bush. "Aren't you even the tiniest bit worried about being able to make him look like a championship cutting horse?"

The man shook his head. "Nah," he said calmly. "If Skye Ransom can have a double, I think it's safe to assume that Skye Ransom's horse can, too."

Stevie clapped her hand to her mouth in astonishment. Then she cried, "I've got it!"

9

"IS EVERYBODY HERE? Whoever's not here, speak up now!" Stevie joked.

"We're all here, Stevie," Carole said shortly. It had been a long, frustrating day, and she wasn't in the mood for Stevie's attempts at humor. All evening Stevie had been giddy with excitement. Nobody could figure out why, and Stevie had refused to explain until The Saddle Club meeting she had planned for that night in the bunkhouse. Now they were all assembled in a circle on the floor, and Carole wished Stevie would hurry up and get to the point. After the disappointing lesson with Skye, she was tired—very, very tired. Kate and Lisa looked exhausted, too.

"Knock, knock. Can I come in?"

Stevie stood up and swung open the door to see who on earth would be visiting them at such a strange hour. "Christine!" she cried. Shrieking with delight, she embraced their old friend, Christine Lonetree, and ushered her inside.

"Hi, everybody," Christine said. "A little bird told me that I might find you here."

"Christine, we haven't seen you around. Where have you been?" Lisa asked.

Christine Lonetree was an American Indian girl who lived near the Devines and was a friend of The Saddle Club. Usually she took early-morning rides on her horse, Arrow, but the girls hadn't seen her yet this trip. They'd been so busy that they'd forgotten to ask for her. Like Kate, Christine was an out-of-town Saddle Club member. She had taught the girls a lot about American Indian culture.

"To be honest," Christine said, "I've been avoiding the place. John told me that it had been invaded. I didn't want to spook Arrow, especially since the reason we take the dawn rides is that it's usually peaceful and we can both relax. But," she added, "I had to come see you guys. Kate called me and told me about the meeting tonight."

"Guilty as charged," Kate said happily. "Christine's bunking with us tonight."

"We're glad you could make it," Lisa said. She scooted closer to Carole to make room for Christine. Christine plunked down on the floor.

"Actually, your showing up is the best thing that's happened all day," Carole said.

Taking turns, the girls filled Christine in on the events of the past few days.

"Boy, I heard Hollywood was ruthless, but it sounds like the director has really gone too far, telling Skye he can't ride," Christine remarked. "What are you going to do to stop him?"

"We don't know," Lisa admitted. "That's the problem."

"We *didn't* know, you mean," Stevie corrected her.

"If you don't tell us your idea within five minutes . . ." Carole threatened.

"Okay, okay. But it's not really *my* idea," Stevie said.

"Then whose is it?" Kate asked.

"The stuntman's! Skye's double," Stevie replied. "You saw him watching today, right?"

"Did I ever! As soon as Skye noticed him, he forgot

how to ride," said Carole. As she had predicted, Skye had been very unsettled by the stuntman's presence. He had tried to act confident, but he hadn't been able to remember a thing.

"Before you all get more annoyed at him, allow me to relay a comment he made this afternoon," Stevie said. "I told him how awful Prize is and I asked him why he wasn't more worried about having to ride him. He said, 'If Skye Ransom can have a double, I think it's safe to assume that Skye Ransom's horse can, too'!"

Stevie should have been used to the long silences that always seemed to greet her amazing news. But she wasn't expecting The Saddle Club's reaction to be quite so listless. Nobody said a word. "Did you hear what I said? A *double* for Skye's *horse?*"

A little timidly, Lisa spoke up. "I know what you're getting at, Stevie, but the thing is, even if Prize could have a double, Stewball could never be it. I hate to say it, but even at a distance, a pinto looks totally different from a chestnut."

"Yes, I think even Blake Pratt, Director, would notice that difference," Carole added.

The group murmured their assent. Stevie rolled her eyes in exasperation. "I *know* that, but how hard can it be to disguise Stewball? This is Hollywood, remember? Anything goes. All we have to do is figure out a way to dye his white patches. How hard can that be? Then we have Skye demand to ride tomorrow afternoon with the promise that he can be subbed out the minute he messes up. It'll go like clockwork!"

Lisa clapped her hands and looked sharply at Stevie. "You know, I think you've got something," she said. "It could work, if we can find a way to get rid of those white spots. . . ."

Lisa's enthusiasm was all that was needed to convince everyone else that Stevie's plan was worth pursuing. Christine, Kate, and finally Carole chimed in, and they began to brainstorm wildly.

"How about Easter-egg dye?" Kate threw out.

"We'd have to buy about five thousand decorating kits," Lisa pointed out. "And it might not be safe."

"What about tomato juice?" asked Stevie.

"Gross!" everyone yelled.

"Magic Marker?" Lisa joked.

The suggestions got sillier and sillier until Christine suddenly got a faraway look in her eye.

"Uh, Christine?" Carole said.

Christine refocused her attention on the group. "A long time ago, the members of my tribe were experts at

94

making paints and dyes from natural materials—plants, flowers, bark, clay. They used the dyes to color all kinds of fabrics, and the men used to paint their faces and bodies for celebrations and war. I read about it in a library book, too. Dyeing was common in many tribes. It was part of the artistic culture, too. I wonder if they ever dyed horses. . . ."

"How did people learn how to make the dyes?" Lisa asked breathlessly.

"The skill was passed on from generation to generation so that it would never be lost."

"Really? That sounds perfect!" Stevie said. "It's at least worth a try. You'll teach us, right?"

Christine looked startled. "Oh, no, I'm sorry. I don't know the first thing about that stuff."

"What about your parents? Do they know?" Lisa asked hopefully.

Christine shook her head. "They don't know any more than I do. My mom makes glaze for her pots, but it's not the same thing. No—the only person who might know how to make the dyes is John. His grandmother taught him when he was little."

As one, the girls all turned and looked at Lisa. "But I can't ask him!" Lisa protested. "I can't! He's just gotten to the point where he doesn't hate Skye and he'll talk to me again, and now I'm supposed to ask him to dye a horse for Hollywood so that Skye gets good reviews?"

"But Skye's whole career could be on the line," said Carole.

Stevie sat forward a little and murmured, "Just picture it: Skye rides in on Stewball, disguised as Sir Prize. The scene goes perfectly. The director stands up: 'It's a take!'"

Lisa let out a long breath. She looked from Stevie to Carole to Kate and then to Christine, who looked puzzled. Briefly she told Christine about John's general dislike of the movie people, his run-ins with the director, and his suspicion that Skye was like all the rest of them.

"I can't say I blame him," Christine said. After a minute she added, "You know, up until a few years ago, most Westerns were very unfair to American Indians. Things have changed now, but it took a long time for Hollywood to come around and realize that there's more to our tribes than scalping, raiding, and pillaging. We were always portrayed as the bad guys. John may have that in his mind, too.

"And don't forget, he's also an animal lover," Christine continued. "Many of the so-called classic Westerns were abusive to horses. They used running wires to trip the horses as they were galloping so that their falls would look

96

realistic. They jumped down from second-story porches onto the horses' backs, and they rode very roughly. I don't know if John has thought about all this stuff, but it wouldn't surprise me."

Christine's points were important, and the girls considered them seriously. Whether or not the history of Westerns had upset John, they were glad that Christine had brought up the subject. It had made them think.

"Would it be wrong of us to ask John to dye Stewball?" Lisa asked. Beside her, Stevie giggled. Somehow Lisa's putting the question into words made it sound comical. In a minute they were all chuckling. After the seriousness of what Christine had said, it was a relief to laugh.

"No, of course not," Christine said kindly. "You can ask him, and he can always say no. It's not as if he'd be selling out by helping you. You're his friends, and *Cowboy, Come Home* sounds like a harmless movie."

Lisa felt reassured by Christine's words. Maybe John would be happy to be in the thick of things, to be a crucial member of the team. Besides, John knew his own mind. He wouldn't agree to do something that went against his conscience. Or would he? If she were the one to ask him? But the whole point was that she *had* to be the one to ask him because she had the best chance of getting him to say yes. It was too late to wonder about it now.

Stevie had taken Lisa's silence for a yes. She had gotten Lisa's bathrobe down off its hook in preparation for a repeat of her evening stable conference with John the night before. "Remember, Lis', there's no time like the present," Stevie said.

"I can't promise anything," Lisa warned them, sticking her arms through the sleeves.

LISA HAD AN odd sense of déjà vu as she headed out to the barn. Once again she had to talk to John. And once again the subject wasn't one that she was eager to bring up. She had been so pleased that John was beginning to be his old self again. She didn't want to wreck it by asking him for too much too soon. For all Lisa knew, she could set off another angry tirade about Hollywood. But she couldn't let her friends down, especially not Skye. She had been involved from the beginning: She was the one who had suggested the Bar None in the first place. It wouldn't be her fault if it didn't work out—if Skye didn't get to ride—but she still owed it to him to try to help.

After nosing around the barn for a few minutes, Lisa found John in Tex's stall. He was putting the chestnut gelding away after grooming him. "We've got to stop meeting like this," John said kiddingly when he saw her.

"I know," said Lisa. "I'm beginning to feel as if we're in cahoots and we're planning some dangerous scheme." *Actually*, Lisa thought, *that's not so far from the truth!* "Wow, Tex looks great," she added. "How was your ride this afternoon?"

"I didn't get to go," John said. "I came back to saddle up Tex, and instead I had to saddle up twelve other horses for the Hollywood spouses' trail ride."

"Oh, no! I'm sorry, John. That's disappointing," said Lisa.

"It's okay," John replied. "They'll all be gone soon and then I can get back to working with this guy." He gave Tex a pat on his glossy neck. "Actually, it was kind of funny. *They* were kind of funny, I should say—the spouses, I mean. We had seven wives, four husbands, and one mother, and not one of them had been near a horse before. It took an hour just to get them mounted. Thankfully, one of the other hands led the trail ride."

Lisa and John chatted for a while longer, and Lisa found herself avoiding the subject she'd come to discuss. But it was getting late, and the others would be dying to know the outcome of her mission. She *had* to say something. Finally, in a long, roundabout manner, after talking about everything else under the sun, she mentioned

Stevie's plan to disguise Stewball. Offhandedly she added, "I hear that many of the American Indian tribes used to have experts who knew about dyeing."

"That's true. My grandmother used to make dyes for blankets, pots—lots of things," John said.

"John," Lisa said in a rush, "do you think they ever dyed horses? Would *you* know how to dye a horse? Or at least dye his white parts?" With her request out in the open, Lisa could only wait for John's reaction.

He thought for a minute. "In answer to your questions: I don't know if they dyed horses, but it wouldn't surprise me if they had; and yes, I know how I'd dye a horse. It's easy. You just—"

"No! Don't tell me! I don't want to know. You don't have to give any kind of tribal secrets away. That would be wrong," Lisa insisted.

"But it's no big se—"

"You might not mind telling now, but you'd regret it later. What I was hoping was that you could do the dyeing yourself," Lisa said, her fingers crossed.

"Sure," said John. "I could do that, but it's not a—"

"You could? I mean, you will! I mean, would you?" Lisa cried, getting flustered.

"Why not? I'm on the technical team, aren't I? Although I guess this would come under makeup, wouldn't it?" John joked.

Without stopping to think, Lisa gave him a huge hug. "Thank you so much, John! You've saved the day!"

John hugged her back. When they separated, he reminded her, "Hey, I haven't done anything yet. When do you want him dyed?"

Lisa thought fast. "Let's see . . . the shoot is at three o'clock in the afternoon, so I guess tomorrow morning. Unless you need more time to collect the plants and berries and things."

"No, I don't need more time. Tomorrow morning's fine. How about nine o'clock?" John said.

"Great! We'll meet you here?"

"I'll see you at nine o'clock," John promised.

THE NEXT MORNING Stevie, Carole, and Lisa raced through breakfast at lightning speed. All three of them had the jitters. They had been so excited when Lisa told them the good news about John that none of them had been able to get to sleep until the middle of the night.

"If Christine hadn't come and told us about John, what would we have done?" Carole asked, gulping her orange juice.

"And what if Kate hadn't called Christine? We never would have come up with the plan," Lisa said.

"What if the stuntman hadn't come to watch Skye ride?" Stevie asked.

"And what if we'd never met Skye in Central Park? And what if I'd never decided to take riding lessons and never met you?" Lisa asked, cracking up.

The whole morning they'd been having silly conversations like this one, out of sheer nerves. None of them could quite believe that everything was going to go according to schedule—that John was really going to dye Stewball, that the director would be fooled, and that Stewball was going to perform as perfectly as he had in the lessons.

After breakfast, Lisa went to Skye's trailer and told him the plan. "It's brilliant!" Skye exclaimed. "You guys are amazing! So all I have to do is show up to ride?" he asked.

"And convince the director to *let* you ride," Stevie answered.

"No problem—he won't deny me one final chance. Not even Blake Pratt would do that!"

AT NINE O'CLOCK sharp the girls reported to the stable. "I thought a couple of us could take a nice little trail ride," John said meaningfully.

The girls had a quick conference and decided that only Stevie would go with John. Two riders would attract far less attention than four. And by staying behind, Lisa and Carole could make excuses for John's absence if anyone asked where he was. John told Stevie to saddle up her horse. "I'm assuming you'll be riding your usual mount?" John inquired pointedly.

Her hazel eyes flashing happily, Stevie played along. "Yes, I think I'll take Stewball. You never know when his cutting abilities are going to come in handy."

As soon as the horses were ready, Stevie and John mounted up. Lisa noticed that John's saddlebags and backpack were bulging. Obviously, the materials for the dye were inside. She and Carole gave Stevie and John the thumbs-up signal and watched them jog away from the stables.

"I want to hurry so that if anyone sees us, it will only be for a moment or two," John called back over his shoulder. "That way there'll be less chance of anyone noticing that one of our horses is a pinto—a pinto who's going to come back as a chestnut."

"Hear that, boy?" Stevie asked Stewball. "You're about to get the beauty treatment of your lifetime."

Instead of taking the usual trail toward Parson's Rock, John made a sharp right at the trailhead and headed in the opposite direction. Jogging and loping when the footing was good, they reached a small creek in about half an hour. Stevie was beside herself with excitement. "I feel like a real horse rustler!" she said. "It's too good to be true."

John was all concentration. "Well, most rustlers probably have a lookout person, so you can be it. I have to ask you to wait over there," he said, pointing to a large boulder. "I doubt anyone's going to come this way at this hour, but yell if you see anyone approaching."

Stevie agreed. Normally she would have tried to finagle a way to go with John, but Lisa had specifically mentioned the night before that they shouldn't try to find out the ingredients of John's concoction. She felt it was important that he be able to keep it a secret.

"I'm going to take both horses down the creek where it's shallower," John explained. "Tex, here, as my packhorse—he's got the supplies—and Stewball, for obvious reasons. I need water for the dye. We should be back in an hour."

"We'd better synchronize our watches," Stevie said, imitating his superserious tone.

John raised his eyebrows skeptically.

"In movies, the criminals *always* synchronize their watches!" Stevie insisted.

"All right, all right!" John said. Under his breath he added, "This *is* for Hollywood, after all."

Their watches set, John led the horses away, and Stevie scrambled up the bank to her position behind the boulder.

The wait was pure agony. The minutes ticked by. Stevie sat, then stood. She counted birds flying overhead. She recited the parts of the horse. She made a Christmas wish list, even though Christmas was six months away. She sat down again. Then she looked at her watch. Exactly fourteen minutes had elapsed. "Aa—" She was about to scream, but then she realized she couldn't, or John might think someone was coming. She stood up again, and, pacing in front of the boulder, she started to sing "One Hundred Bottles of Beer on the Wall."

When an hour and six minutes had gone by, she heard a familiar whinny. She sprang out from behind the rock—and saw an utterly unfamiliar horse. It was Stewball, but he was a chestnut! The transformation was unbelievable. "John, you're a miracle worker!" Stevie screamed. Now was definitely not a time for understatement.

John smiled a bit sheepishly. "It was nothing."

"Nothing? Are you kidding? It's amazing!" Stevie said. "It's the most incredible thing I've ever seen."

"No, *really*, it was nothing."

106

Fine, Stevie thought, *let him be Mr. Modest about it. The point is: The plan's going to work!* "Can I touch the dye?" she asked.

"Sure, it won't come off," said John. "But we'd better be getting back. Lisa and Carole will be wondering where we are, and I've got real chores to do."

Gingerly patting Stewball on the neck, Stevie swung back into the saddle. On the ride back to the barn, she kept leaning forward and back to stare at Stewball's previously white patches. Up close, she could see a vague difference in the shade of the chestnut that had been white and the real chestnut patches, but it was nothing the camera would pick up twenty, ten, or even five feet away. In spite of her promise to Lisa, Stevie was aching to ask John what had gone into the dye. Somehow she managed to keep her word. She did make a mental note to try to research American Indian dyeing techniques in her school library come fall. There was no telling how many ways such a powerful dye could come in handy for pranks and practical jokes.

LISA AND CAROLE had almost the same reaction as Stevie. They stared at Stewball in shock. "John, this is—it's—it's beautiful," Lisa breathed.

"I'm glad you said 'it's' and not 'he's,' " Stevie said loy-

107

ally, "because I, for one, think Stewball was beautiful before, in his natural state."

"What's funny is that he doesn't look anything like Sir Prize," said Carole, "even dyed the same color. Any horseman or horsewoman could tell the difference in a second; the horses have completely different conformation. Stewball's back is shorter, his neck isn't as broad, he—"

"Yes, Carole?" Stevie interrupted. She knew that when Carole got going about horsey stuff, she could go on forever.

"Oh, right. What I was going to say is that luckily the director won't notice the swap in a million years."

"Let's hope you're right," Lisa said. For some reason, she felt more cautious about the success of the plan than Stevie or Carole.

"I wouldn't worry about the director," John said. "Heck, Skye could probably show up riding a chestnut cow and get away with it. Now, listen: Today is taken care of. And so's tomorrow. The dye should last till Friday. After that, though, we're going to have to rinse it out and redye."

"Stewball's scenes may be finished in a couple of days. According to Skye, Blake wants to fly everyone out this weekend," Stevie said.

"If that's what happens, great. But otherwise, remember that it won't last forever, okay?" John said.

Before John left, Lisa took him aside and thanked him again. She began, "I don't know what to say—"

"Then don't say anything," John whispered. He reached down and gave her hand a warm squeeze. "I was happy to do it."

CAROLE GRINNED AS she led Sir Prize out of the huge stall in his private barn. "Come on, you big oaf, it's time for you to disappear."

The animal trainer was waiting outside. "Now, you're sure Mr. Ransom wants you to put the tack on Sir-Sir?" she asked nervously.

"Yes, I'm sure. Didn't he come tell you?" Carole asked, feigning innocence.

The woman nodded, keeping pace with them. "He—he did, but I always like to double-check."

Carole walked faster to discourage the woman from following. "Mr. Ransom will personally return his mount after the shoot," she said.

"All right, I—I guess," the woman said, finally dropping back. "Take good care of him! He's a very valuable animal!" she called.

In the main barn Carole found an empty, out-of-the-way stall. It was a straight stall, not a box stall, which meant the horse had to be tied standing forward. The ranch hands used the straight stalls when they needed to keep a horse on hand temporarily—before the farrier's or veterinarian's visit, for instance. A straight stall was completely safe and acceptable as long as a horse didn't have to live in it around the clock.

"I'm sure these quarters are shockingly small for you, Sir," Carole said as she tied Prize's lead line to the ring on the wall with a quick-release knot, "but I'm afraid it's the best we can do for our supporting cast this afternoon. You see, your understudy is about to take center stage."

THE FRONT ROW of chairs on the viewing platform was deathly quiet. Carole, Stevie, Lisa, Kate, Christine, and John were waiting for the scene to begin. A hundred yards away, Skye was mounted on Stewball. All they could do now was cross their fingers and hope.

The director's nasal voice carried over the whispered conversations of the crew and the other viewers. "Too bad this probably won't be the final shoot," he said to a cameraman. "Those dark clouds add just the right touch of menace for this scene." After another minute or two, the director gave a signal to one of his assistants.

"Quiet on the set! Quiet, please!" the assistant yelled.
"Five, four, three, two, one—roll film!"

They saw the cattle first. Moving at a lively pace,
the cows and calves came toward the corral. Then Skye
and Stewball appeared, herding them like old pros,
with the sheepdog running alongside. And it was just
as Stevie had said: The whole scene went like clockwork.

Stewball may have been a chestnut, but underneath he
was the same quick, clever cow horse he'd always been.
He jogged, he loped, he stopped, he turned on a dime. He
anticipated the herd's every move, and Skye gave him free
rein to do it.

Skye himself sat boldly on top, his cowboy hat fixed at a
rakish tilt. Together, and with the dog's help, they
brought the cattle into the corral. When they were all
penned, Skye clanged the gate shut and herded them
down to one end.

Lisa stole a glance at the director. He was staring, utterly transfixed, at the scene.

Skye backed up and chose a calf to cut. He galloped
toward the herd, sending most of them stampeding to
the other end of the corral. But one calf was caught, fac-
ing off against the horse and rider. Skye let Stewball

show his stuff as he prevented the calf from joining the herd. Then, with a loud whoop, Skye let the calf go. He took off his cowboy hat and tossed it high in the air.

"Cut!" the director screamed. "It's a take!"

EVERYBODY JUMPED UP and raced onto the set, shouting happily. The Saddle Club high-fived one another as they ran to surround Skye. "It's a take! It's a take!" Stevie yelled.

Skye jumped off and started hugging people. "I owe it all to you guys!" he said. "And you!" He gave Stewball a hug.

"And we owe it all to . . ." Lisa looked around for John. She couldn't see him anywhere. It was just like him to leave before taking any credit. She would have to catch up with him later.

"John's gone?" Carole asked. She had to yell to make herself heard above the celebratory din.

Lisa nodded. "I'll bet he went to do some work."

"He's not going to get away with this!" Carole said. "We're going to publicly humiliate him with praise!"

"You'd better believe it," Skye said.

The director was standing a few feet away, talking with crew members. "Now, that's what I call a real cutting horse. That Prize is incredible. I may not know much about animals, but I can always recognize talent."

Grinning delightedly, The Saddle Club winked at one another.

"Say, we'd better pack it in, Boss," said one of the men. "It looks like it's going to rain."

Even as the man spoke, the first drops began to fall. The storm that Frank Devine had been following in the paper had finally arrived.

"We might as well pack it in, too, huh?" Stevie said. "I'll ride Stewball back if no one minds."

"Yes, let's get him put away, so we can do the swap again," Carole said. "If he gets all wet he'll—oh, oh, ohmigosh!" She had been about to say "He'll be harder to cool down." But suddenly John's words came back to her. And they came back to all the girls at the same time.

We're going to have to rinse it out and redye. John had dyed Stewball with a water-soluble dye.

There was a momentary pause in the rain. It was the calm before the storm. It lasted about two seconds. Then the drops turned into a deluge, and Carole began to yell. "Quick! Stevie! Get him out of here! Hurry! Hurry! Before it's too late!"

But it was already too late. Stewball sidled away from Stevie, stubbornly refusing to let her get on. The rain poured down. The girls covered their eyes. And in a matter of minutes, Stewball was a skewbald once again.

EVERYBODY BEGAN TALKING—or shouting—at once. The Saddle Club demanded to be heard. The director demanded an explanation. Skye demanded to talk to his manager. The animal trainer demanded the real Sir Prize. The crew demanded to get out of the rain. And every so often, Stewball let out a loud, triumphant neigh.

Finally there was a break in the uproar, and the director's high-pitched voice won out. "Look!" he whined. "All I wanna know is how fast can we sign this animal?"

Skye translated for the girls. "Stewball's hired!"

"Then may I suggest, on behalf of Stewball, that we all adjourn to the stables where it's dry?" Stevie asked.

"Do you work for me?" the director asked.

"Not exactly," Stevie replied.

"Well, you oughta—that's the best idea I've heard all day," the director said.

THE GROUP TROOPED over to the stables. Carole took the animal trainer to Prize's stall. "My poor baby!" the woman cried. "He's suffocating in this tiny stall. It's an outrage!"

Prize surveyed the two of them with a bored look. Then he opened his mouth and yawned, a huge horse yawn, with all his teeth showing. Giggling, Carole went to join the others.

While the girls gave Stewball his rubdown, the director took out a cellular phone and began making calls. "You got any coffee around here?" he asked when he had hung up.

"Nope. Sorry," Stevie said. "And frankly, I don't think we should talk coffee before we talk contracts. So, why don't you sit yourself down on that bale of hay there and make my client an offer."

Lisa and Carole had to bite their tongues to stop themselves from bursting into laughter. All of a sudden, Stevie had picked up the Hollywood lingo and was talking like a mogul.

Looking chastened, the director did as he was told. He

116

perched gingerly on the bale. "Look, I'm not sure I can make an offer right away," he said. "There's a lot to consider, after all. I can't just—"

"Actually, Blake, there's only one thing to consider, and that's my client's career. A horse like him doesn't come around very often. Now, if you want to hem and haw and beat around the bush, that's fine. But Stewball is a busy horse. He doesn't have time to wait around. Carole, Lisa—put him away."

"Wait!" the director cried, springing up. "Okay! I'll do it! I'll have my people get in touch with your people tonight! We'll have the contracts drawn up right away."

"That's more like it," Stevie said.

"Once all parties have signed, you'll have to go and talk to makeup as soon as possible," the director continued. "I don't want any delay in shooting the other couple of scenes."

"Makeup?" Stevie repeated, taken aback. "Why should I talk to them?"

"Why, to tell them how to do the dye job right. We're still going to use Prize for the close-up head shots, naturally. So we'll want Stew, here, to look as much like him as possible. Just like today."

After a moment of panic, Stevie decided to come clean right away. She still had the upper hand, and if she played her cards right, she could keep it. "There's only one person who knows what's in that dye," she declared.

"What do you mean, one person?" the director asked.

"The dye is an ancient, secret American Indian tribal concoction that has been handed down for generations." Stevie shot a worried glance at Lisa, begging for help.

"That's right," Lisa chimed in. "The only person who knows the formula is the boy who dyed Stewball this morning." More than anything, Lisa wished John were there to hear again how important his role had been.

"Hey, listen, don't give me all this 'ancient, secret recipe' stuff. Just get me the kid, okay?" the director said.

"That might not be as easy as it sounds," Lisa said truthfully. John had been happy to help them out today, but Lisa wasn't about to ask him to put himself out again.

"Look, I'll hire him, too, okay? What does he want? Money? He's got it. His own makeup studio? Done!" the director said.

"What about creative authority?" Stevie demanded.

"Fine—that, too! Anything! Just get me that boy! *Get me that boy!*" With that, the director gathered up his things and made his exit out into the rain. Soon The Saddle Club could hear his cries of "Coffee! Someone bring me coffee!"

"Just what he needs," said Lisa. "More caffeine to make him more high-strung and jittery!"

"Now, now. Don't be too hard on Blake. Underneath it all, he's a decent guy," Stevie said, reclining on the hay bales to savor her success.

"Let me guess: You're contemplating a career in directing now," Lisa said.

"Nope—acting. I figure I deserve an Oscar after that performance."

Lisa and Carole didn't know whether to agree with Stevie or smother her with hay. It truly had been an award-winning scene. They were saved from the decision when Kate appeared in the doorway.

"Listen, I want to hear all the details, but I can't talk now. I came by to tell you that dinner is a barbecue up at the house. It's raining so hard that it can't keep up. The minute it stops, we start grilling. Mom and Dad want to thank everybody for all the hard work they've been doing," she said in a rush.

"Great!" Carole said. "We'll be there."

"If you see John, make sure he knows about it, will you? We can't find him. And tell Skye he's invited too, okay?" Kate asked. "I've got to go chop tomatoes for salsa!"

"She forgot the most important guest," Stevie said, sitting up. Stewball was dozing on the cross-ties, tired out after his first day on the set. Stevie stood up and scratched his back where he liked it most. "Funny how you wouldn't let me get on when the rain started, wasn't it?"

"Stewball's not the type to wait in the wings," Carole said. "He saw his chance for stardom and took it."

"What do you say we make our starlet beautiful for the barbecue and then go out and do a rain dance?" Stevie suggested.

"But a rain dance is what you do when you're praying for rain," Lisa pointed out. "We've already got the rain."

"Then we'll do a reverse rain dance," Stevie said. "Or something like that."

"You two go ahead," Lisa told them. "I'm going to go find 'that boy.' "

12

KATE HAD BEEN RIGHT about the rain. It rained so hard that it rained itself out. By the time Lisa left the stable to look for John, it was barely drizzling.

Lisa searched high and low but couldn't find him. She checked in all the main ranch buildings, she walked out to the corrals and back, and she asked everyone she saw. She stopped by the Devines', but Phyllis Devine told her that everybody was so busy getting ready for the barbecue that John could easily have slipped in and out without being noticed. "Good luck!" she said to Lisa.

After going back over the territory she had covered,

Lisa decided to stop by Skye's trailer. She wanted to tell him about Stevie's run-in with the director and make sure that he knew about the cookout as well. When she rapped on Skye's door, she heard laughter and conversation inside.

"Lisa! Come on in!" Skye said when he opened the door. "The more the merrier. John and I were just saying we should go find you girls."

"John and you?" Lisa said, not believing her ears.

"Hi, Lisa!"

As Lisa's eyes adjusted to the dim light in the trailer, she saw, to her amazement, John relaxing on Skye's couch. "Come sit with me," John said.

In a daze, Lisa went and sat next to him. "Boy, I didn't expect to find you here," she said.

Both John and Skye laughed heartily. "I didn't expect to find myself here," John said.

"You took off so fast after the shoot that nobody had time to thank you," Lisa said.

"I've already told him he's in trouble for that," Skye said. "He's not allowed to save the day and then take off ever again."

"I didn't mean to!" John protested. "But after the scene was over, I realized it was going to rain any second. Tex and a bunch of other horses were out in the corral with no

122

shelter. At first I was going to let them get rained on, but then I felt bad, so I sprinted over to get them inside. You can't blame me for that, can you?"

"No, I *guess* not," Lisa said. In fact, that was one of the reasons she liked John so much: He always put horses, animals, and other people ahead of himself.

"Then I was going to run home and change, but instead I ran into Skye," John continued.

"Right. We looked like a couple of drowned rats, so we hightailed it back here to dry off," Skye said.

Lisa had been so happy and surprised to see John in Skye's trailer that she hadn't noticed he was wearing Skye's clothes, too. "Hey, nice shirt, Skye," she said, looking admiringly at the navy blue polo shirt John wore. She didn't mention that it looked especially nice on him.

"Thanks. It's a good color, isn't it? I wonder if you could *dye* something that color, John," Skye said pointedly. The two boys burst into hysterical laughter.

"What's so funny?" Lisa asked, perplexed. "I'll bet there are natural blue dyes, aren't there, John?"

When he could catch his breath, John replied, "Probably. But not in the women's hair coloring section of the drugstore!" He and Skye began to laugh uncontrollably again.

Lisa looked from one to the other of them. *"What did you say?"* she asked.

John wiped tears from his eyes. He cleared his throat and attempted to look serious. "I'm sorry, Lisa, but I didn't use an American Indian dye to turn Stewball chestnut."

"You didn't?"

John shook his head. "Uh-uh."

"What did you use?" Lisa asked.

"Color-Me-Gorgeous Temporary Dye in Luscious, Lustrous Red."

"What?" Lisa said again. "You mean women's hair dye?"

John nodded sheepishly.

"But what about the secret dye?" she asked. "What about the ancient traditions?"

"For one thing, those techniques aren't secret," John said. "I tried to explain, but nobody would listen."

"But when I asked you—"

"All I said was that I thought I knew how to dye a horse," John said gently.

Lisa thought back, but she couldn't remember the conversation exactly. All she could remember was being worried that her request would upset John. "So you don't know how to make natural dyes and paints?" she asked, feeling a little deflated. "Christine thought your grand-mother had taught you."

"She did. I do know a few things. I could dye a shirt or a piece of fabric. But the natural dyes would be too weak to color a horse. At least, I think they would. I've never tried. And it just seemed so much easier to run down to McNab's Pharmacy and stock up on Luccious, Lustrous Red."

At the name, Skye began to chuckle again. John couldn't help himself, either. And as she watched the two of them cracking up, the humor of the situation suddenly hit Lisa, too. "So, do you mean to tell me that the whole time we thought you were guarding a tribal secret, you were off buying home dye kits?" she demanded. "Why the heck didn't Stevie, Carole, Kate, Christine, and I think of that? What are we, total idiots?"

"I do have to confess that I kept up the act with Stevie," John said. "When we went to dye Stewball, I acted all serious and I wouldn't let her watch me do the job."

"Normally she would have watched anyway," said Lisa, "but I strictly told everyone not to try to find out the secret recipe or bother you about it at all. I'm never going to live this one down!"

Even though John laughed, Lisa could tell he was touched by her admission. In a dry voice, he said, "Thanks for worrying about me, Lisa. And while I'm confessing, I might as well apologize, too, and get it over with." Skye gestured that he didn't need to go through with it, but John said, "No, it's important to me to say this. I acted like a real jerk, to both of you. I did exactly what I accuse other people of doing—I didn't make judgments about people as individuals. I massed everyone together in my mind as 'Hollywood.' I'm sorry I let that get in the way of meeting you, Skye."

"You were pretty darn rude," Skye admitted. "But since I have ten or twenty encounters like that every day, I hardly noticed, to tell you the truth." The boys grinned at each other.

"Hey, speaking of rude people," Lisa said. She launched into the story of The Saddle Club's encounter with the director, detail by unbelievable detail.

"It's a good thing John didn't fess up before now!" Skye said when she had finished. "I can't wait to see the director have to grovel to John because he's the only person who's capable of redyeing Stewball. If he only knew!"

"I hope Stewball will still talk to me, now that he's going to be famous," John joked.

"Sure he will," Lisa said. "You're his personal hair-dresser now."

"The animals in this movie get better treatment than the human actors!" Skye told them. "Prize's stall is bigger than this trailer."

They looked around the cramped room, strewn with clothes, scripts, and dirty cups. "And he probably eats better, too," said Skye, holding up an empty SpaghettiOs can.

"I almost forgot!" Lisa exclaimed. "You're both invited to a barbecue at the Devines', starting"—she glanced at her watch—"starting now."

"A barbecue? You mean a real Western barbecue with chicken and ribs?" Skye asked.

"Chicken and ribs?" John said. "That's only about one-tenth of the food the Devines will put out."

"Yippee! Today really is my lucky day," Skye said.

"Yours and Stevie's," Lisa replied. "She's probably planning to break some kind of eating record tonight."

"Why don't we all head over, then?" John suggested.

Skye started to agree and then seemed to change his mind. "You two go on over. I'll be there in a few minutes. There are a few things I want to take care of."

John went back into Skye's bedroom to get his things.

"Are you sure you don't want to come with John and me now?" Lisa asked.

Skye nodded, his eyes twinkling. "I'm positive. You and John should go alone. Take a nice, leisurely walk over. I'll be there soon."

Lisa looked at Skye, astonished. Had he guessed about her and John?

"Hey, I may be an actor," Skye whispered, "but that doesn't mean I don't notice real feelings."

"Okay, Lisa. What do you say?" John asked, standing on the threshold.

Lisa beamed, first at Skye and then at John. "I say let's hit the barbecue. We deserve it!"

"See you there, Skye?" John asked.

Skye nodded. "See you there."

OUTSIDE, THE RAIN had ended. Lisa looked up. There were a few big, billowy, fair-weather clouds dotting the brilliant expanse of blue. In the west, the sun was just beginning to set over the Rockies. She and John walked side by side. All at once Lisa felt awkward and very conscious of John's presence.

"You're right, you know," John said finally. "Skye's a great guy. He's modest, funny, down-to-earth—nothing like what you'd expect from a big teenage star." He paused for a minute. "You know, I said in there that I lumped Skye together with all the other Hollywood people, and that's true. But I guess I separated him, too—I mean, since he was your—your friend."

"We're all friends with Skye," Lisa said.

"I know, but . . ." John seemed to be having trouble continuing.

"I—I do like Skye a lot, John, but, um, only as a, well, as a friend," Lisa managed to stammer out.

John let out a huge sigh of relief. "I was hoping you'd say that," he said.

So it was true! Lisa thought. John had been jealous of Skye! "You were?" she said.

"I sure was." Instead of elaborating any further, John took Lisa's hand in his. He didn't let it go until they got to the barbecue. Lisa blushed so hard she thought her face was going to go up in flames.

When they got to the Devines', Stevie and Carole ran up to meet them. "Come on, you guys! You have to go say hello to the guest of honor!" Stevie cried. "He's the Bar None's newest heartthrob—Stewball!"

THE COOKOUT WAS a wonderful affair. All the girls stuffed themselves to their hearts' content. Skye and John stuffed themselves, too. About halfway through dinner, Carole

noticed a small man lurking on the fringes of the party.
"Say, isn't that the director?" she asked.

They all turned to look. Blake Pratt waved hopefully at
them.

"I know why he's here," Stevie said. To the director she
called, "Come on over!"

"I don't want to interrupt, but I thought perhaps I
might be able to speak with Stewball's, er, hair consultant?"

"I'm the consultant," John said.

The director nearly jumped out of his skin. "You're the
consultant?" he said.

"Yes," John said. "I'm the consultant. I'm also the cof-
fee-bringer and the dogcatcher, as I'm sure you remember."

The director grimaced. "I thought I recognized you," he
said resignedly. "Look, I was in a horrible mood on both
of those days—and the dog *could* have killed me! If I
seemed rude—"

"It's okay," John said.

"It's okay?" the director and The Saddle Club cried in
unison.

"Yes," John repeated, "it's okay. We all have bad days
once in a while—days when we don't act like ourselves."

130

He looked directly at Lisa, and she nodded understandingly.

"Right!" the director said. "That's what I was trying to say. Now, about Stewball's dye job . . ."

WHEN THE FOOD was almost gone, Frank Devine stood up and waved his hands for silence. "I know there's been a lot of extra work getting ready these last few weeks and coping with the Hollywood presence this week. You've all been great. I just wanted to thank you and let you know that part of the Hollywood money will show up in everybody's paycheck as a nice-sized bonus at the end of the month." Frank smiled at the loud cheers that greeted his announcement.

"Now, I'll let you get to your brownies in a minute, but first I want to thank two boys in particular. One of them is an employee of mine: John Brightstar. He worked harder than I thought possible all week, but all of it was behind the scenes. That's the way John is. He doesn't show off, he just gets the job done. And I'm told he's responsible for turning our own crazy old Stewball into a movie star. Which brings me to the next boy. Some of you asked me tonight if this barbecue was for Bar None people only, and I said yes. You might have been surprised to see Skye

Ransom, the star of *Cowboy Come Home*, joining us for dinner. Well, I'll tell you why I asked Skye to come: He may be a Hollywood star, but over the past few days, he's become a Bar None person, too. I don't think I need to say more. You've all gotten to know Skye because he made an effort to get to know you. He's made this show run a whole lot better than it would have without him. So, Skye, let me tell you: Cowboy, forget going home. You can stay right here if you want! Now let's eat dessert!"

As if on cue, the crowd rose and burst into applause for John and Skye. Stevie, Lisa, and Carole cheered the loudest. When the clapping had died down a bit, Stevie turned to her friends. "Now, that's what I call a Hollywood ending!"

13

"SAME OLD SATURDAY night," Stevie said listlessly. It was a week after the girls had returned from the Bar None. Stevie was still suffering from the let-down feeling she always had after an exciting trip. She had invited Lisa and Carole to her house for a sleepover to try to get out of her blue mood. "No movie stars, no horse swapping. You know, I even miss Blake Pratt, Director. He sure livened things up."

"No, we don't exactly have those things, but we do have this," Lisa said. She pulled a video tape out of her overnight bag. "Of course, it's way too early for the movie,

133

but Skye sent me some clips of the filming they did on the ranch."

"Go ahead and load it!" Stevie urged, switching on the TV and the VCR.

Lisa popped the tape in, and they all settled back on the Lakes' living room couch to watch. A card flashed across the screen. In black marker it said Cowboy, Come Home, with a bunch of numbers and dates.

"They should have called it *Stuntman, Go Home*," Stevie joked.

"Was he ever upset!" Carole recalled. After having been flown in from Los Angeles, Skye's double had been dismissed as soon as Frank Devine had signed a contract for Stewball.

"Little does he know that it was his own fault he didn't get to ride," Stevie said.

"Shhh—they're on!" said Lisa.

The girls watched, enthralled, as the scene they had watched in real life unfolded on the screen. It had already been edited and touched up, so it looked very professional—nothing like the home movies Stevie liked to make of her brothers clowning in front of the video camera.

"I can't believe we really know him," Lisa breathed, starstruck all over again by Skye's on-screen persona.

"Who, Stewball?" Stevie said, feigning innocence. "Why, he's just a little ole cow horse."

"Ha, ha," Lisa said. "And anyway, that's not true anymore. Stewball's famous . . . sort of."

"Do you think he'll find ranch life boring now that he's 'gone Hollywood'?" Carole asked.

"I think Stewball will always find ranch life just fine—anywhere where there's a calf to cut or a cow to herd," Stevie said, her voice choking up a little. Even though it had been great to ride Belle again, she missed Stewball.

The girls clapped when the scene ended, then laughed when the film cut to a close-up of Sir Prize looking off into the distance. "At least he can prick his ears up pretty well," Carole said.

Stevie went to stop the tape, but Lisa told her to wait. "I think the preliminary credits are here, too."

Sure enough, music swelled on the sound track and the credits rolled. They all watched until Kate's and their own three names, as well as John's, came up under "Technical Advisers." John Brightstar was also listed under "Makeup." And under "Stuntman," there was only one name: Stewball.

"Did Skye say anything about his upcoming projects?" Carole asked.

Lisa shook her head. "No, he's not sure what's next. When I said good-bye to him, he just said, 'Until we film again.' "

"And what about John?" Stevie inquired. "What did he say?"

"Oh, we're planning to keep in touch," Lisa said nonchalantly.

Stevie and Carole didn't push Lisa to talk about it. They knew that sometimes sharing every last detail with friends could make something less special. They could guess that Lisa's good-bye with John was something she wanted to keep to herself for now.

"Do you think he'll ever teach you what's in the special dye?" Carole asked, her voice dreamy.

Lisa bit her lip. "I kind of doubt it," she said.

"Maybe the next time we go out West, he'll take you berry picking and show you what plants are the best, and how to mix them to get just the right hue," Stevie said, imagining a romantic scene.

"I'm not so sure about that," Lisa said.

"Because the techniques are too complicated?" Carole asked gravely.

"Not exactly," Lisa said. She took a deep breath. "Have you two ever heard of Luscious, Lustrous Red?"

ABOUT THE AUTHOR

BONNIE BRYANT is the author of many books for young readers, including novelizations of movie hits such as *Teenage Mutant Ninja Turtles* and *Honey, I Blew Up the Kid*, written under her married name, B. B. Hiller.

Ms. Bryant began writing The Saddle Club in 1986. Although she had done some riding before that, she intensified her studies then and found herself learning right along with her characters Stevie, Carole, and Lisa. She claims that they are all much better riders than she is.

Ms. Bryant was born and raised in New York City. She still lives there, in Greenwich Village, with her two sons.